LOVE, DIE, NEIGHBOR

A PREQUEL IN THE KIKI LOWENSTEIN MYSTERY SERIES

JOANNA CAMPBELL SLAN

spot on publishing

CONTENTS

Joanna Campbell Slan/Spot On Publishing

9307 SE Olympus Street

Hobe Sound FL 33455

http://www.joannacampbellslan.com

Publisher's Note: This is a work of fiction. Names, characters, places, and incidents are a product of the author's imagination. Locales and public names are sometimes used for atmospheric purposes. Any resemblance to actual people, living or dead, or to businesses, companies, events, institutions, or locales is completely coincidental.

Love, Die, Neighbor/ Joanna Campbell Slan. -- 1st ed.

To All My Readers –

When I began this series, I had no idea how many wonderful people I would meet through Kiki. Thank you, thank you, thank you. You mean the world to me!

Your friend,
Joanna

~

Note: *In the timeline of Kiki's life, this books comes before* **Paper, Scissors, Death** *(Book #1 in the Kiki Lowenstein Mystery Series).*

PROLOGUE

My life in crime began with a good deed.

You see, I dialed 911 after a neighbor took a tumble off his racing bike. Under the right circumstances, contacting the emergency dispatcher would have been a normal response to Sven Nordstrom's cry for help.

But Sven's accident didn't happen under normal circumstances. It happened after a series of nasty interactions between our family, the Lowensteins, and his, the Nordstroms. There was definitely bad blood between us.

When Sven took that fatal fall, my behavior as a concerned citizen linked me to his death in ways I couldn't begin to imagine. Rather than prove my good intentions, my cry for help looked suspicious. The ugly finger of blame pointed my way.

That's how I, Kiki Lowenstein, became involved in a murder investigation.

1

My husband, George, and I took possession of our new house the minute it was habitable, on the Friday before Labor Day weekend. We literally walked in as the construction crew walked out. We were that eager to get settled. The technical term for this is "beneficial occupancy," but in retrospect, it should have been called a "big mistake."

We should have waited another week and allowed a cleaning crew to thoroughly vacuum, dust, and scrub all the surfaces. But after six months in a cramped extended stay hotel, the three of us were desperate to get out of each other's way. This house would actually allow us to go for weeks without bumping into each other. But first, we'd need to get settled in.

The interior of the four-thousand-square-foot building looked like the aftermath of a natural disaster. Sawdust thickened every surface. Loose nails and screws had been scattered everywhere. Drywall dust covered all the woodwork. Dirty footprints marred the tile floors. The wooden floors looked dull, thanks to a film of ground-in dirt. Stray pieces of lumber rested precariously against the bannisters and walls.

In the midst of all that mess sat enough boxes to fill an entire moving van. All our worldly belongings had been packed in cardboard containers of all sizes. The stacked boxes towered over my head, in many cases giving me a surreal sense of existence. In the dim light, I could imagine visiting Stonehenge, where the stone monuments dotted England's landscape.

"Job One is setting up Anya's playpen," I told my husband. "Otherwise, I don't know how I'll keep her from hurting herself. Once that's done, I can dig in and try to sort out this mess."

"Right," my husband George said. "Once we get the playpen and the high chair, you can get to work doing your job, and I'll get back to mine."

My job. It would feel good to be productive.

George and I had met at my first (and last) frat party at college, where I learned that drinking Purple Passion Punch is the first step on the path to losing your virginity and getting pregnant in one fell swoop. When George found out I was expecting, he immediately offered to marry me. Faced with a lot of bleak choices, I took him up on his offer. Once we'd tied the knot, there was never any question of living anywhere but here —St. Louis — George's hometown.

At the ripe old age of twenty-two, I'd gone from college sophomore to newlywed, from living in a dorm to a small apartment, here in "the Lou." The Lowensteins had deep roots here. Their connections allowed George to go into business with an old friend from high school. Together, the men opened a real estate development company.

That partnership allowed us to build this honking big house, a regular McMansion at four thousand square feet on a big lot in Ladue, the swankiest town in the metro-St. Louis area. George acted as our subcontractor, borrowing crews from other jobs. This saved us a lot of money, but it also meant that building our house took longer than expected.

"Just think," George had said. "This will be the perfect place for Anya to grow up. She'll have everything her heart desires."

I had agreed. Our child had definitely been born into a life of privilege.

"Okay!" George rubbed his hands together. "While I'm at work, bringing home the metaphorical bacon, your job is to get this place cleaned up and make new friends in the neighborhood."

2

_A_ week after our move, a brisk knock on the front door announced my first visitor, Sheila Lowenstein, my mother-in-law.

"Good morning and welcome," I said.

"Come here, precious." As usual, Sheila ignored me to reach for my baby.

I yielded Anya without complaint. Balancing the toddler on one hip, Sheila walked past me. Her denim blue eyes scanned the mess. She wove her way between the towers of boxes and gave the place a quick inspection. "You have a real mess on your hands."

"Yup."

"Please don't talk that way. My granddaughter will pick up bad habits."

I clamped my mouth shut and nodded. Sheila intimidated me. Often her criticisms echoed a voice in my head that urged me to adopt a higher standard. To an outsider, I was caving in. More truthfully, I was making a course correction.

"Too bad you couldn't have had this place professionally

cleaned before you moved in. You can't possibly let Anya wander around in all this debris."

I'd never heard anyone use "debris" in casual conversation, but there it was again: Sheila was right.

"We set up her playpen, her crib, and her high chair. I've got her stroller in the trunk of the old BMW. She's properly corralled. Of course, she wants to get down and explore, but I won't let her."

"Most women in your position hire cleaning ladies, but those people also have active social lives. In fact, a great many of them volunteer in various capacities. If you'd like, I could put in a word for you. I know of a symphony committee that would put your skills to good use."

"That sounds promising," I said. In my head, I imagined writing press releases or doing interviews. After all, I'd been a journalism student before dropping out of college.

"So you're willing?" Sheila planted a kiss on Anya's cheek.

"Um, could you tell me more? I'd like to know what I'm volunteering to do exactly, before I firm up a commitment. "My acceptance was less than whole-hearted, because my experiences with Sheila had proved she didn't think much of me. Although I needed the company of adults, I doubted I'd be joining them on an equal footing — especially if my introduction came from my mother-in-law.

Quickly and sadly, I learned how right I was.

"There's a public relations committee meeting tomorrow night at my house."

My spirits soared. *Wow.* Sheila was really coming through for me!

She continued, "While we discuss our plans, you can stuff envelopes. We have two thousand of them we need to get out. Oh, and they need folding, too."

Crash-landing. Boom. My ego smacked up against reality.

"Oops. I'm busy tomorrow night. Anya will need a bath."

If that sounded petty, well, Sheila deserved it.

"Suit yourself." She heaved a sigh of relief.

I did the same. I had little desire to subject myself to the scrutiny of Sheila's friends, who ran various boards. While I admired her for giving of her time to good causes, I knew I wouldn't fit in. With a job, I might garner their respect. With grunt work, I'd only encourage them to think I was the village idiot. Their village idiot. Sheila knew it, too. Her smile was oiled with insincerity.

"You will need to find some way to get involved in the community. Otherwise how will Anya make friends? You don't want her to be an outcast, do you? She'll only have you to blame."

That stung. Criticizing my popularity or my housekeeping skills was to be expected. But questioning my ability as a mother? That was another thing entirely.

As I fumed, Sheila's mouth settled into a snarky Mona Lisa smile. Zinger sent. Target hit. Score: One for Sheila, and zero for Kiki.

The jabs Sheila launched in my direction never failed to score a direct hit to my soft belly.

I loved Anya more than life itself. The thought of her hurting herself on a bit of construction trash that had been left behind nearly paralyzed me with fear. Sheila had pounced on my greatest challenge — keeping Anya safe. I chewed the air, wondering how on earth I could manage to clean up the piles of sawdust, find all the scattered nails and screws, mop the filthy floors, wipe down the dusty woodwork, and unpack all our boxes from the apartment.

The answer: I couldn't.

3

"We've only lived here a week," I reminded myself, after waving goodbye to Sheila and opening the door to the heating and cooling contractor. He banged away merrily at our unit, whistling as he worked. Smiling down at Anya, I said, "I'm getting things done, but it takes time, doesn't it, pumpkin?"

My baby grinned at me. "Bird?" she asked. Recently, she'd learned that word, and now she was making full use of her newest vocabulary addition. Each time we went outside, she scanned her surroundings for a winged creature.

The boxes and mess nagged at me, but the world outdoors issued an irresistible siren's song. I'd gotten accustomed to the banging and clanging, but the blasts of alternating hot and cold air irritated me.

"I've had enough. How about you? Should we go outside and look for birds?"

"Yay!" she cheered. I loaded Anya in her stroller for a walk around the block.

Once out on the sidewalk, I heard bike tires eating up pavement — and I froze in place, waiting to locate the source of the noise. Every morning for the past week, Sven Nordstrom had whirled out of his garage on his fancy racing bike, only to return an hour later.

"He's a semi-pro bike racer," George had told me, after he had walked over and introduced himself. "Can you believe that bike weighs less than 15 pounds? Anya weighs nearly as much. He rides an Orbea Orca M-TEAM Road Bike, with a super light-weight carbon fiber frame. It costs more than $6000. Sven is in training for a big race. He told me that he covers six to ten miles every day, rain or shine, and he clocks himself."

I admired the man's discipline. Since Sven left about the same time George headed to the office, I'd witnessed our neighbor's reliability first-hand. When it came to his daily bike ride, Sven Nordstrom was a well-oiled machine.

Turning my head, I spotted him turning the corner into our cul-de-sac. He was right on time. As I walked Anya to the side-walk, the bike zipped past me. "Bird?" Anya pointed to a wren hopping around on the mud pit that would eventually become our lawn.

"Yes, sweetie," I said, but I couldn't stop myself from frowning. "Bird" and his friends were eating our grass seed. No wonder nothing was sprouting in the wet dirt. I would have to talk to George about this. He'd been counting on seeing new grass push through to the surface.

After making a mental note of the problem, I watched Sven out of the corner of my eye. Rather than take his usual sharp right and speed into his garage, he hit the curb, hard.

"Oh!" I clapped a hand over my mouth.

His bike came bouncing back, as it slammed into the concrete step and jolted to a stop, whereupon he promptly fell over with a clatter of metal against the pavement. Rather than immediately jump up, he stayed there on the ground and groaned.

Turning the stroller, I pushed Anya across the street.

"Sven? Are you okay?"

Although the man didn't know me — except to wave in passing, a result of George's having gone over and introduced himself — I knew he should recognize me as his neighbor.

"Sven? I'm George's wife. Are you all right?"

He didn't respond. In fact, he made no move to unclip his shoes from the pedals. His eyes seemed unfocused. He kept a frozen grip on the handlebars. It was as if a witch had cast a spell over him and locked him into place.

"Let me help." I stepped away from the stroller and grabbed at the bike frame, hoping to lift it away.

That provoked a reaction. "Don't touch my bike!" he screamed at me.

As I jumped back, he struggled to extricate himself from the tangle of tubes, wires, and spokes.

"Are you sure you're okay?" I ignored how rude he'd been. I figured he was shaken up after the fall and annoyed by losing his balance.

"Perfectly fine." In a smooth reverse squat, he rose to his full height, using the bike for balance. With one hand, he removed his helmet. The nicely chiseled chin and bright blue eyes contrasted with a healthy tan. A full head of blond hair gave him a youthful look, but up close, I could see the crinkles around his eyes. On closer inspection, I detected gray hairs among the gold. That said, the man had an enviable physique, and his tight biking clothes showed off every inch of it.

"If you're sure you're okay..." I paused. "I'm only trying to help. My name is Kiki. I'm George Lowenstein's wife, and I live across the street. If I can do anything for you, let me know."

He closed his eyes as if to get his thoughts gathered. They snapped open as he said, "I never lose my balance. Ever. Don't know what came over me. Usually I ride and don't break a sweat. Today I'm drenched."

"Maybe you're coming down with a bug." Instinctively, I looked him up and down, as if I could assess him visually and tell what was wrong. But when I got to his tight biking shorts, I blushed and averted my eyes. "Anya had a bit of a cold last week, " I added, lamely. Actually, I suspected all the sawdust in the air had bothered her.

"I am never sick." Either he didn't like kids, or he was too rattled to care. Most people remark on how gorgeous my daughter is. Sven didn't seem to notice.

Brushing an errant piece of grass off his leg, Sven mumbled, "Hit me all of a sudden. Got dizzy. Sick at my stomach."

"Sounds like the flu." I had no idea whether it was or not, but that's what I'd overheard people saying at the drugstore. I was doing my best to make polite conversation. "As I said, you've met my husband, George. I'm Kiki. This is our daughter, Anya."

"Right." Clicking the two pieces of his chin strap together, he hung his helmet over the handlebars. "I know who you are."

He still didn't react to my beautiful daughter. Maybe he was one of those folks who just doesn't care for kids.

"Your neighbors," I said again, for emphasis.

"Right," he repeated himself. But the word seemed like a rallying cry, rather than a confirmation that all was well.

As he wobbled past me, I caught a whiff of masculine sweat. Even though I was still standing there in his driveway, trying to make conversation, our visit was over. With his back to me, Sven opened the refrigerator in the garage, grabbed a bottle of Gatorade, and chugged the contents without offering one to me.

I turned to go, stopped, and hesitated, realizing I might never get another chance to ask my burning question. "Is there some reason you leave your garage door up all the time?"

"What are you talking about? We never leave it up. Not ever.

Do you think I'd leave an expensive bike like this out in the open? Where anyone could steal it? Don't be stupid."

Wow.

"I was only wondering. Didn't mean to offend." With that, I pushed Anya back across the street. Moving at a fast clip, I hoped to put Sven Nordstrom and his nasty behavior behind us.

So much for making friends. At least I could tell George that I'd tried.

4

Maybe I'd caught Sven at a bad time. Perhaps he'd been embarrassed by falling off his bike. I did my best to control my emotions by setting off at a brisk pace for a walk around the block. Getting Anya's buggy up and down, over the curbs, and along the sidewalk provided her with endless entertainment and me with great empathy for the handicapped. A couple of times, grabbing the stroller and hoisting it over an obstacle seemed nearly impossible.

Anya wasn't that heavy. The stroller wasn't that big. But, together, the task proved challenging, especially when the stroller wheels touched down on a flat surface before I had the buggy fully under control. At one point, a wheel jammed into a crack between two paving stones. At first, I tugged and tugged on the handle. Next, I squatted down and pulled directly on the tire. Finally, I straddled the front of the stroller, bent over, and tried to jerk the wheel free.

"What ho?" A masculine voice shocked me into losing my grip. If a hand hadn't reached out to steady me, I would have tumbled to the ground.

"Are you stuck?" asked a tall man with a sprout of white hair in the middle of his bald pate. Although he leaned on his cane, he seemed sturdy enough. His black lace-up shoes appeared oddly formal, since his pants were corduroy. The maroon cardigan he wore had been buttoned wrong, a problem that happened to me all the time.

"The wheel."

"Right. I'll get it out of that hole for you. You get behind the pram. Make sure it don't topple over, will you?"

I did as told. Anya blinked up at the stranger. She observed, carefully, as he used his cane like a lever and popped the wheel free.

"Thank you so much. I'm Kiki. Kiki Lowenstein. This is Anya. We live around the corner."

"Talbot Bergen. Where'd you say you live?"

"Ours is the new house. Actually, it's still under construction. In fact, I'm glad to meet you, Mr. Bergen. You're the first person I've officially met in this neighborhood."

Okay, I suppose you could count Sven Nordstrom, but I'd decided to make a fresh start of it.

"Oh." Momentarily, Mr. Bergen looked confused. "Alma takes care of all that. She drops by when folks move in, and invites them over for dinner."

"That sounds lovely. We'd love to meet our neighbors. My husband, George, has been pushing me to get acquainted with everyone. Is Alma home right now?"

"Alma?" I assumed he was talking about his wife.

"What's this little girl's name again?" Either Mr. Bergen hadn't heard me, or he wanted to change the subject.

"Anya. Her name is Anya."

"I had a grandmother named Anya. Pretty name for a pretty girl." As a punctuation mark, he patted my daughter on the head.

"Which house is yours?" I asked.

"That one." He shuffled closer to a gray ranch with dark green shutters. From the design, I could tell it was one of the older, original houses in this subdivision.

"Kitty!" Anya's chubby finger pointed toward a black shape in the window. "Kitty, kitty!"

Mr. Bergen chuckled. "That's Bartholomew. Do you like cats?"

"Kitty. Me-ow." Anya grinned up at him. Her two newest teeth were on full display.

"She loves animals," I said. "Loves them. Absolutely nuts about them."

"Good old Bart! What a rascal."

"He's Persian, isn't he? Beautiful."

"You'd think he was prissy, wouldn't you? But he's not. He loves to slip out and explore. Especially loves to prowl in that empty lot. Yes, ma'am, Bart is a small-sized panther. Meant the world to..." Mr. Bergen wiped his eyes with the back of his hand.

"Talbot?" The voice came from a woman in brown knit slacks and a tired beige sweater. She came hurrying down the sidewalk with us in her sights. Her reddish hair was set off nicely by gold jewelry, but on closer inspection, it looked like very inexpensive costume stuff. "Talbot, dear, here you are. I've been looking all over for you." With a possessive air, she slipped her arm inside of his.

"Hi," I said. "I'm Kiki Lowenstein, and this is Anya. Are you Alma?"

"Not Alma." Talbot's eyes moistened.

"Enid James," she said, but she didn't offer me her hand. In fact, she didn't even look my way. The softness around the jowls and the crow's feet suggested she might be in her sixties, and, once upon a time, she might have been a looker, but the years had run roughshod over her. However, she'd clearly taken great pains with her appearance. Her hair had been died a rich shade of red, and it brought out the gold flecks in her eyes.

"This here's my new neighbor." Talbot sounded proud to introduce me.

"Really?" Enid gave me an up-and-down examination. She wasn't unfriendly, but she was definitely judgmental.

"Just moved in," I said. "Across from the Nordstroms."

A shift came over her, like a cold front blowing in.

"Leesa and Sven. The perfect couple." Enid practically spat out the words, before gripping Talbot's arm more tightly. "You don't know how worried I was about you, Talbot. You don't want to catch a chill, do you? Let's go back to the house. Your favorite programs are on. We can play gin rummy, if you want."

"Goodbye," I said, as they turned away from us.

"Bye-bye!" Anya waved, but they didn't seem to care. Enid and Mr. Bergen seemed to be in their own world, a transparent bubble that separated them from the rest of us.

5

Ten days after we moved in, and three days after I tried to help Sven Nordstrom get up off of the ground, our house was still a disaster. My plan to whip it into shape had proved a non-starter. Workers still needed access on a daily basis. Various switches didn't work. "Mud" needed to be applied to the drywall. Blinds had to be measured, fitted, and installed. Each day brought a parade of new faces, wearing dirty shoes that marched in and out.

Of course, George didn't see any of this, because he left for the office each morning. When he came home at night, the look on his face told me he was disappointed in how little progress I was making, cleaning and picking up.

But he had no idea how tough it was to take care of an active little girl, answer questions, respond to deliveries, make decisions on the spot, unpack boxes, make meals, and then only then, try to clean up the messes left behind from construction. The parade of strangers totally unsettled me. By nature, I'm a shy person. When I get excited about something or when I am comfortable, I can talk a blue streak. Plunk me down in a new situation, and I tend to freeze.

My low self-esteem was exacerbated by the fact I knew I didn't look my best. All of my hair products had disappeared in the scramble of our move, leaving me looking like the wild woman of Borneo. I was still carrying extra baby weight, and none of my clothes were stylish. Anya had grown more demanding, the house was a constant nagging problem, and I never put on make-up anymore.

After settling Anya in her playpen after our walk, I got a glance at my reflection in the mirror hung over the mantelpiece. My lack of personal care was evident. I gazed at the distorted image and shook my head. Maybe I'd scared off Sven Nordstrom and the kindly Mr. Bergen. Something had to be done, and done quickly.

I ducked into a powder room and slicked my hair down with water. Belatedly, I realized that I didn't have a towel. Bent over the basin, I twisted my hair to squeeze out the water. That helped a little, but my curls were still dripping wet when the doorbell rang.

"Hello?" I opened the door to a stranger in a suit and tie. I thought that he wore an air of irritation as he stared down his nose at me. But perhaps the water streaming between my eyes made it hard for me to see him clearly.

"Mrs. Lowenstein, I presume? I'm Jeff Colter. Your neighbor on the other side of the block. Big red brick two-story."

"Hey, so good to meet you. Come on in. I can offer you coffee —"

"This isn't a social call, Mrs. Lowenstein." He straightened his tie. "I wish that it was. I came in response to complaints."

"Complaints?" I echoed.

"That's right. I'm the president of the home owners association, so all the calls come to me. People are sick and tired of the ongoing problems caused by your construction."

That knocked me for a loop. The peculiar layout of this

subdivision had been one of the reasons we'd overpaid for the lot. No one could be bothered by the commotion but the Nordstroms — and since the Nordstroms were hardly ever home during the day, how could we be disturbing them?

Maybe I'd insulted Sven's manhood by offering to help him after his tumble. Was that even possible?

"I can't apologize enough that we've been a bother," I said to Mr. Colter. "The good news is that they tell me they're almost done. A day or two at the longest. We'll just have one guy come back over to handle the punch list and the nail pops."

"Punch list? Nail pops?" Mr. Colter raised an eyebrow. "Won't that be noisy?"

"Not really. A punch list is a list of all the small stuff that doesn't work right. Nail pops are a natural occurrence. As a house settles, the heads of the nails tend to rise. Typically, a workman comes back and knocks them down. Since my husband was our subcontractor, it's been —"

But Mr. Colter wasn't interested in hearing more about our situation. "The long and short of it seems to be that this nuisance will come to an end. Am I right?"

"Yes, absolutely. If you'd like, I can speak directly to the people we've upset and apologize —"

"No." He cut me off yet again. "They asked to remain anonymous. I'll report that the work should be finished soon. If there's any change or delay, I'd appreciate a heads-up phone call."

With that, he handed over his business card. I took it, but I didn't get the chance to look it over. A whimper from Anya in the next room warned me that she needed my attention.

"Thank you. I will." I moved to shut the door, but he stopped me.

With a deadpan expression, he said, "Welcome to the neighborhood. Oh, and I trust you plan to do landscaping? Your lawn looks like a mud pit."

6

*W*hen George came home that evening, I told him about Mr. Colter's visit. "I never realized we were causing a problem. Our house isn't on the main drag. I have no idea why anyone would complain."

"It had to be the Nordstroms," George said. "They're the only people who could possibly be bothered by the workmen coming and going. No one else is close enough to be disturbed."

"That's what I thought, too."

"I think you need to go over and play the peacemaker. That's how Mom would handle it."

I couldn't imagine Sheila soothing troubled waters instead of ruffling feathers, but mismatched analogies aside, I got the point.

"Look, I tried to be nice when he fell off his bike, and he was not very friendly."

"Would you be, if you'd just fallen in front of a new neighbor? If you were this hotshot biker and you took a nosedive in front of the woman who lived next door?"

I certainly wouldn't have acted like Sven did. Thanks to his curt behavior, Mr. Bergen's weirdness, Enid James' frosty reception, and Mr. Colter's ultimatum, I was definitely not eager to meet more people in the neighborhood. But George stared at me with an endearing eagerness. I wanted to please him, so I gave in. "Okay, all right. Do you know anything else about him and his wife? Conversation starters? What does he do for a living? Does she work outside the home?"

"Sven's a software designer. He developed a popular program, sold it, and now he's working on a new one."

"And her? His wife?"

"Her name is Leesa. She's younger than he is. I believe she's an exercise instructor. She looks like she's solid muscle," George said, as he went over to our front window and glanced across the street. "At least, I think I heard somewhere that she teaches classes."

A little voice inside my head heard my husband adding, "And you, my wife, need to lose a few pounds. Maybe she will help you get into shape."

Okay, he did *not* say that, but I imagined he did.

Since giving birth to Anya, I'd gone from rounded to roly-poly and from soft to squishy. I tried to look at my body as infrequently as possible. The inflated inner tube of fat around my waist embarrassed me.

"Has their garage door been open all day long?" George peered through our blinds at the Nordstrom's house.

"Yup. I asked Sven about that. He told me I was nuts."

"Hmmm. Maybe she's leaving it up, and he doesn't realize it. I hate looking straight into their clutter."

"Me, too." Day in and day out, we were treated to a view of their cars, their bikes, their shelves, all their various car and lawn chemicals, and their garbage and recycling bins.

"Anya and I met a sweet, little old man. Mr. Bergen. He and his wife Alma live in the gray house with the green shutters."

"That's nice," George said. "I bet that's Talbot Bergen, the chemist. You've heard of Bergen Laboratories, right? Has to be the same guy."

"Anya was particularly taken with the family cat, Bartholomew. He's beautiful."

"Don't even think about suggesting we get a pet."

It was as if he'd read my mind. Anya got her love of animals from me. I'd never been without a furry pet, and George's refusal to even consider a dog or a cat was a source of conflict between us.

"Good for you, meeting the old man. All I'm asking is that you make an effort," George said. "That's all. You should introduce yourself to more people. It would be nice for us to have new friends."

I promised I would.

7

*B*ut the very next morning, something happened that made me rethink that promise.

George had come home for lunch, because he planned to talk to a landscaper about the ugly mess that should have been a lawn. The guy didn't show; however, the three of us had an enjoyable family meal of grilled cheese sandwiches and tomato soup, an absolute favorite, especially in the fall.

The weather was beautiful, a perfect day with a light breeze and the promise of cooler air on the way. Instead of simply walking George to his car, I decided to pop Anya in her stroller and take her for a quick tour of the neighborhood. Meanwhile, George walked over and waited by the driver's door, making a big deal of waving to Anya and shouting, "Bye-bye."

Because of the way my husband had parked his Mercedes Benz, I couldn't get the stroller between the vehicle and the garage door. Instead, I had make a detour, walking behind the back bumper. We didn't swing out far, but two of the stroller wheels were in the street.

Suddenly Sven and his bike came whirling out of his garage and into the cul-de-sac.

A sprinkling of rocks on the pavement had been left behind by the many workers' trucks. Sven must have hit one, because I heard a funny noise, a cross between a crunch and a scrape. Turning toward it, I watched with horror as Sven lost control of the bike and headed straight for Anya.

"Hey!" George screamed.

"Stop!" I yelled.

"Move!" Sven responded.

Grabbing the stroller handlebar, I struggled to lift my child up and out of the way. But the combination of the angle and her weight defeated me.

Sven was still headed toward us. In a herculean effort not to hit Anya, he threw all his weight to one side and screeched to a sliding halt. The bicycle tires screamed in protest, while he locked his brakes and skidded in a half-circle. For a heart-stopping second, it looked like his back tire would still slam into Anya's front bumper.

At the last second, I jerked the stroller backward. But Sven had come so close to hitting it that Anya and I could both feel the whoosh of air that he had created. Anya sucked up air, filling her lungs. Her lower lip quivered.

But before she could bellow in fear, George came flying into the street the way an Olympic runner launches himself out of the block. With one hand, he grabbed Sven's handlebars, hauling man and bike to an upright position. "You almost hit my daughter!"

On cue, Anya screamed so loudly that my ears hurt.

"Let go of my bike." Sven snarled at George and gave him a sulky glare.

Leesa stepped out of their house. Shaking her fist, she approached us. "You was in street!"

George made a sound surprisingly like a growl.

"This would never have happened," said Sven, "if your stupid wife hadn't pushed your kid into the street."

Plucking Anya out of the stroller, I rocked her in my arms. She was working herself up into a real tizzy. It registered that I'd been called "stupid," but my daughter's needs were uppermost. "Sh, sh," I said as I tried to comfort her.

George and Sven stared at each other, like two stray dogs sizing each other up. Leesa stopped at their curb, her eyes darting from one man to the other.

Fortunately, for all involved, the confrontation ended abruptly, as Anya let out a particularly plaintive howl. The ear-splitting wail from her lips distracted George. He turned around to check on her. His change of direction allowed Sven to ride off into the sunset...sort of.

8

"That idiot nearly hit my grandchild? With his bicycle?" Sheila's eyebrows rose toward her hairline. In her slender fingers, the ruby colored wineglass glowed like a precious gem, thanks in part to the Sabbath candles. The starched white tablecloth and heavy silver candlesticks added elegant touches to our Friday night meal. "That's outrageous. However, the man was right. Kiki had no business pushing the stroller into the street. That near miss would have never happened, if she'd been more careful."

We had dinner at Sheila's house at least once a week, usually on Friday to celebrate Shabbas. My mother-in-law was a recent widow; her husband Harry had been dying of cancer when I met George, and the older man succumbed shortly after. Sadly, he had not lived long enough to meet Anya, but Harry had left such an impression on me that I would never forget him. He had been wonderfully kind and welcoming. Spending time with his grieving wife was my personal attempt at honoring a man whose memory was a blessing.

Often I said nothing during the meal, except to compliment Linnea, the Lowensteins' longtime housekeeper, on the food, which was always exquisite. Linnea cooked up a storm, and her beef brisket was unusually delicious. More to the point, the kindly black woman doted on me. Whatever portions I particularly liked, she would wrap up for me to take home as leftovers. Although I loved everything Linnea cooked, I did have my favorites. She made a bread topped with caramelized onions that was out of this world, her creamed spinach became my favorite dip for chips, and her pies often found their way onto a plate for my breakfast.

"Kiki, it won't do for you to make enemies of the neighbors," Sheila scolded me. "George does not need enemies. He's growing a business. Your job is to make friends. Who knows? The Nordstroms might be well-connected in the Swiss community. One of their friends might want to buy a house in one of George's developments."

"Sven and Leesa are Swedes, Mother. Not Swiss citizens." George could correct his mother with a winning smile, whereas I tended to mimic one of Linnea's briskets and stew in my own juices.

"That's irrelevant, darling boy." Sheila tossed back the last of her Malbec. "Point being that your wife should act as the family's ambassador."

George obediently poured her more wine and refilled my glass, too, even without asking.

I lifted my goblet to my mouth to cover my smile. Sheila's suggestion that I should make friends for our family's sake was ironic. Although we'd only lived in the metro-St. Louis area for two years, I'd already encountered more than a handful of people who'd gotten crosswise with Sheila and lived to tell a tale of woe. In fact, I'd been at a library function, a book club event, when another patron asked, "Lowenstein...as in Sheila?"

When I nodded, she turned to her companion, a woman

who'd listened to my response with a shudder. Shortly after, the two friends got up and left with one backward glance at me.

"You are willing to make amends, aren't you, Kiki? I can trust you to cross the street and extend an olive branch, can't I?" Sheila's frosty stare was totally at odds with the warm red of the wine in her glass.

"Right," I said, turning my attention to Anya, as she chewed on a hunk of Linnea's homemade bread.

"Please give me a real answer, Kiki. Not a nebulous evasion."

"Right, as in, yes, of course, I'll offer myself as a human sacrifice to Sven the spin-meister. I'll even do it at my earliest convenience."

Sheila allowed herself the tiniest unladylike snort. "Since your personal calendar is so full, I'll expect to hear about your visit before we meet for dinner next week. Won't I?"

I meant it as a smile, but I had the feeling my grin had faded into a smirk, as I said, "Right."

9

That night, I had trouble getting to sleep, thinking about another meeting with the Nordstroms. When I did doze off, I had awful dreams. I pictured five-foot-two me as a supplicant to our neighbors while they towered over me like ancient Amazonian figures. I woke up full of gratitude that it had only been a bad dream, and that my whimpers didn't wake up George.

The wine must have done a number on me, keeping my brain from sinking into a restful slumber. Not that it mattered. Tiny crinkling noises broadcast by the baby monitor signaled that Anya was wide awake. As I hauled myself out of bed, her thin voice cooed in a secret language all her own. I suspected she was jabbering to her stuffed toy, Mr. Blue Bunny, or having a serious conversation with the mobile of stars and moon shapes that waltzed slowly over her head.

No matter whether I was well-rested or not, my daughter needed me. Parents don't get to call in and take a day off. As always, the sight of her filled me with such an unbearable ache of love that it nearly knocked me to my knees. How could one small person have become my entire existence? I couldn't even imagine life without her. She was the sum total of my reason for living.

Picking her up, I vowed to do all I could to give her the best life possible. I had no choice but to give in to her grandmother's demands to become the family ambassador. (Or scapegoat, depending on your point of view.)

Once Anya was ready for the day, and I'd changed into street clothes, we went downstairs to the kitchen for our breakfast. In the middle of the table was a note from George, explaining he'd had an early morning meeting and reminding me of Job One: *Try to smooth things over with the Nordstroms.*

To his credit, he went on to say, "Okay, we didn't ask Sven to ride around like a maniac, but let's be the bigger people. I want to enjoy our home for years to come. Getting along with the Nordstroms will be a step in the right direction."

I sank my head into my hands and stared at the walls of boxes piled around me. "Oh, good. Anya? While I was sleeping, everyone took a vote. The Nordstroms are now officially my problem. Isn't that terrific? Not only am I responsible for you, for unboxing this stuff, and for cleaning up this mess, while doing laundry and making sure there's food on the table, I get to offer myself up as a human sacrifice to the Nordic gods across the street."

With a sigh, I continued, "We all know that I am so outgoing and charismatic that this little task shouldn't be any trouble at all. Right, sugar bear?"

She crowed and banged her fork on the tray of her high chair.

"I don't think I can face a bowl of cold cereal. I don't think I can plow through these boxes to find a clean coffee cup. In fact, I know I can't. Tell you what, how about if we go for a ride?"

She tossed the fork over the side of her high chair. It hit the floor and bounced between two boxes.

"I'll take that as a 'You go, Mom!' Love the way you simplify decision-making, little girl." I tugged her out of the high chair and balanced her on one hip. "I mean, here I debate what's a good course of action, while you move boldly ahead with a purpose. I could take lessons from you, Anya. In fact, I bet that's why you're here. To teach me stuff."

10

_I_ have my child perfectly trained. We know the way to every McDonald's in the city, and we can even find the route to a few out in the boondocks, too. Anya catches sight of those golden arches and the chanting begins, "Do-no, do-no, do-no." As I turned into the drive-through lane at the restaurant nearest our home, her cheers grew louder and louder.

After I received my order — two sausage burritos and a large coffee for me, an English muffin and an orange juice for her — I found an empty spot in the parking lot. There we ate our food. Thus satiated, we tossed the trash into a can and headed for Whole Foods, a local grocery specializing in organic and healthy fare. It wasn't my usual place to shop, but I'd worked it out in my head that only the best would do for Sven and Leesa.

Because I badly needed a dose of courage to face the Nordstroms, I decided to take an approach with proven success. I would arrive on their doorstep like the proverbial Greek bearing gifts. Maybe I'd be more warmly received. I bought an expensive, gluten-free, über-healthy chocolate cake, paired with a bouquet of fragrant fall mums and asters, and a cheery "Hi, Neighbor!" card that I signed: _Kiki, George, and Anya Lowenstein._

How could anybody resist the wonderful peace offerings I had planned for the Nordic gods across the street? Anticipation of their delight boosted my self-confidence. While the tantalizing smell of chocolate begged me to sample the treat to make sure it was worthy, I resisted the urge. Instead, I drove us straight home after shopping.

After lifting Anya out of her car seat and bringing in the goodies, I dressed my daughter in her cutest outfit. I ran a brush through my hair and secured it in a clip. After washing my face, I added a smear of lip gloss. Satisfied that I looked passable, and she looked adorable, I carried Anya down the stairs.

She fought me as I loaded her into her stroller. At twenty-six months, she struggles to assert her independence, a sign she's growing up. As much as possible, I encourage her, but today I was on a mission. Into the stroller she went.

A nip in the air signaled fall was in full swing. I picked our way down the mud-splattered concrete driveway, along the side-walk, across the street with its smattering of gravel, and up our neighbors' pristine brick drive.

The Nordstroms' yard presented a stark contrast to ours. Their front lawn looked plush as a thick green carpet. Their landscaping was mature, perfectly proportioned to their house, while our spindly shrubs seemed cheap and puny, as if we'd tossed a handful of twigs into the soil willy-nilly.

"Give it time," I reminded myself. "Home wasn't built in a day."

Anya grinned, her new front teeth gleaming in the sun. She had roared into toddlerhood with a vengeance. Her new favorite words were, "No" and "Wha-da?" The latter being her personal code for, *What is that?*

"Friends," I told her as we bumped along. "Next to family, they're the most important part of life. In fact, I venture to say that in my life, they could easily outrank family. If I had any. Friends, I mean. You have family, Anya, but...it's complicated."

In response, she tossed her Blue Bunny off the side of the stroller. I quickly retrieved the stuffed toy and brushed it off. After a guilty look around to see if anyone had noticed this lapse in hygiene, I handed the blue toy to Anya and pressed onward.

"Here goes Operation Make New Friends," I said to Anya as I stepped under the Nordstroms' portico. The small, open air porch sheltered the front door, but did not invite visitors to "sit a spell and relax." Its purpose was totally utilitarian, a way of blocking precipitation.

Taking a deep breath, I pressed the doorbell. From the back of the stroller hung a reusable fabric grocery bag festooned with dancing fall leaves. My mouth fairly watered as I thought about the cake inside. Paired with a fresh bouquet of fall flowers in jewel-tone colors, I hoped my gift would be irresistible. The scent of the flowers formed a delicate counterpoint to the rich fragrance of chocolate.

The door crept open a sliver. I craned my neck to take in a perfectly oval face framed by a wheat-colored sheath of hair. Leesa Nordstrom towered over me by nearly twelve inches. The woman was built like a runway model, with legs that never seemed to end, and a figure anyone would envy. Especially an "anyone" like pudgy, post-baby fat me.

"Yes?" Leesa's lilting accent rendered the word foreign to my ears.

"Hi! I'm your neighbor Kiki Lowenstein, and this is my daughter, Anya. We haven't been properly introduced so I wanted to drop by and say hello."

Immediately behind Leesa, Sven's face appeared. He ventured a tentative smile, but his wife's expression did not change. Her eyes did not even glance at my adorable daughter. Instead, she drilled an iceberg stare into my forehead.

"Lowenstein. That's what? Jewish?" She spoke slowly as if the words caused her pain.

My mouth fought to keep the smile steady. "Yes, it is. I was born Episcopalian, but my husband and Anya are Jews."

"Hmmm." Her posture stiffened.

Sven did an about-face. I watched the back of his head retreat into their house.

"This is for you." I extended the goodies toward Leesa. "Chocolate cake. From Whole Foods. And flowers."

"We do not eat sweets. The colors of the flowers do not match our decor."

Okay. Two gifts rejected, one to go.

Digging around in the bag, I dredged up a greeting card. "Here."

With two fingers, she extracted the offering from my hand, but the icy expression on her face didn't change one bit.

11

"*D*arling." Sven appeared as if conjured by a magician. He announced his presence by lightly capturing Leesa's shoulder with one hand. "Give this woman a chance. She is trying."

Yes. My mother often said that: *Kiki is trying. She's a test sent by God to torture me.*

Although the words stuck in my throat, I said, "Sorry for all the inconvenience you suffered during the building process."

It seemed to me, and I could be wrong about this, that our roles were reversed. The Nordstroms should be welcoming us to the neighborhood, not the other way around. However, in the name of harmony, I was willing to humble myself.

"This has been big, big problem. Costs us extra money. Makes so much trouble. I must now give new cleaning lady more money. So much work she does. All because of you." Leesa pouted like a child.

At that point, turning tail and taking a hike back home seemed immensely appealing.

But Leesa was on a roll. "Your people block our street.

Spread much dirt. Ruin grass. We chose quiet place, and you make everything noisy. We don't like."

"Right." I nodded automatically. Agreement is always safer than voicing opposition.

Over his wife's shoulder, Sven gave me a look that suggested he didn't want to get involved. I didn't blame him. But that left me standing there and taking her complaints like the punching bag I was becoming.

At that point, I would have laid odds that Leesa was a kickboxing instructor. I could feel the blows to my midsection.

"Sorry about the hassle. It was never our intention to inconvenience you."

"A card is stupid." With a sneer, she dropped the envelope back into my bag. However, her aim was poor and the lovely card toppled to the ground.

That was the last straw.

Bubbling up inside came the voice of rebellion. My psyche was invaded by an angry little goblin, who is normally kept under lock and key. I bit my tongue, but I guess I didn't chomp down hard enough, because the words tumbled out, "Gee, who'd have thunk it? Who would have guessed you'd have a bit of inconvenience when you bought a house across the street from two lots that were for sale? It probably came as a real surprise that anyone would buy a prime piece of vacant property and build on it. Maybe you thought it would stay undeveloped forever? Of course, if you'd paid one bit of attention to the property values, you would know that didn't make sense. But you didn't, huh? What a shocker. And you think that card is stupid."

If I hadn't already turned my back on the Nordstroms, Leesa would have slammed the door in my face.

I seethed with anger on the short march home, and I burned to tell someone how rude Leesa had been. But George didn't walk into the house that night until eight, long after Anya had fallen asleep in her crib. Powered by the energy of anger, I'd done three loads of laundry and emptied four boxes. I quickly became discouraged, as the cardboard cartons proved to be full of my husband's sports equipment. Putting his gear away would be pointless, as he was very picky about his things.

In the end, I gave up on tidying up. Instead, I tried my best to get interested in a new book but found that tough sledding. When George finally walked in on me, I was sprawled on the living room sofa. He asked, "How'd the visit with the Nordstroms go?"

And I told him.

But the sympathy I'd expected was not on the menu.

He shook his head. "You do realize you made things worse, don't you? Why? Maybe Leesa Nordstrom just needed the chance to vent. Now you've gone and gotten yourself new enemies. What happened to your grand idea about finding new friends?"

"I found one today."

"What's her name?"

"Gluten."

"Gretchen?"

"*Gluten.* Gluten-free chocolate cake."

12

*T*wice a week Sheila called me without fail. By contrast, I never heard from my mother. She hadn't called or sent a card since Anya arrived. Although the conversation with Sheila often annoyed me, I couldn't fault her for not caring.

"How is the unboxing process going?" My m-i-l sounded truly interested.

"Not good. We still have workmen coming in and out. The grass seed hasn't sprouted like we thought it would. The workers keep tracking in mud. As for the boxes, I'm doing my best, but George is gone a lot. I don't want to put away his things without his input."

"Have you managed to clean up the sawdust and the rest of that junk?"

"Nope. I make a small bit of headway each day, but with men coming back all the time, I'm not making any progress. My biggest priority is Anya. Keeping her happy and safe. She's curious about everything."

"That because she's a smart child. You can always tell. The

dumb-dumbs sit there like lumps. The intelligent ones explore their environment every minute."

I winced. Sheila's heartless correlation between activity and intelligence upset me. My mother-in-law could be blunt to the point of hurtful. I only prayed she didn't share these unkind thoughts with anyone but me.

"You need a cleaning lady," she continued.

"Yes, I know I do."

"Then get one!" With that, she hung up.

After putting Anya down for a nap, I hopped to it. The task proved harder than I'd expected.

Sylvia Pujoli, the real estate agent who found this lot for us, seemed like a great place to start. "I wish I could help you. Really I do. But I've had my own cleaning lady for decades. I'm out of touch with people who do that sort of work."

"Even if I could find someone to help temporarily, it would make a huge difference. With Anya being so active, I can't step away from her long enough to clear the mess left by the construction crew."

"I warned George that having you move in without getting the place professionally cleaned was a mistake," said Sylvia. "Especially with a toddler in the house. But he wouldn't listen. Now you're paying the price."

After that, I tuned the woman out, because instead of helping me clean my house, she was trashing my husband. "I told George...blah-blah-blah," she said, over and over. I let her ramble, while I folded clothes.

But I stopped my activity, when she added, "George told me that he's decided to bring in Lilly Lansky, the interior designer. I explained to him that she's hard to work with. Runs right over people. He didn't pay one bit of attention. Says your mother-in-law is sold on Lilly. Is that true?"

"I have no idea. I didn't even know he'd contacted a decorator."

"Don't let her hear you call her that. The proper term is 'interior designer.' At least, that's what they want folks to say. Call her a decorator, and she's likely to paint your walls a ghastly shade of pink, just for spite."

"Okay, thanks," I said. "That's good to know. Hey, I think I hear Anya. Have to go! Bye!"

Ending the call filled me with a deep sense of relief and an equal portion of loneliness.

Okay, who else could I call about finding help? Certainly not Sheila. She hadn't hired anyone in ages. Linnea, the Lowensteins' maid, had worked for them for decades. But Linnea might be able to connect me with a friend or two. She belonged to a big A.M.E. (African Methodist Episcopal) Church, and not surprisingly, Linnea had tons of friends among her fellow church-goers.

"Laws, child. There used to be a lot of women who wanted positions. We took pride in our work. Young people today think that being a domestic helper ranks right down there with share-cropping. I'll ask around at church, but don't count on me, hear?
"

I thanked her and booted up the old computer George had set up in the spare bedroom. There I found all sorts of ads for cleaning services. Most seemed to offer crews. That was both good and bad. If I relied on a crew, there wouldn't be a problem if one person got sick or quit. But I remembered what a disaster it had been, when George hired a cleaning crew to help out in my ninth month of pregnancy. Six of them stood around in our kitchen and fought over who had to clean the toilets. When they finally decided on a division of duties, each person hurried to finish without caring what sort of job she'd done. The halls that connected the rooms were still in need of attention.

A few of the outfits advertising online handled catastrophes. I wondered if we qualified for that. Our situation seemed borderline to me. Reading further, learned these businesses tidied up after suicides, natural disasters, and bloody crimes. Although I love reading murder mysteries, I never stopped to think about the messes that happen as a natural result.

Gee whiz, and I thought I had problems.

"Gross," I told Anya. "That's a level of service we don't need. Not yet at least."

I read the names of cleaning concerns to her: Quicker Picker Uppers, Maid to Order, and Clean as a Whistle. None of them inspired confidence. They all sounded frivolous. I made a few calls, but I wasn't willing to hand over my credit card until I knew I'd found the right crew for us.

There had to be a better way to find a cleaning lady.

Then I remembered the bulletin boards at Kaldi's Coffee. Didn't people advertise services there all the time?

Bingo!

Any excuse for a visit to Kaldi's was a good one, but now I had a super-duper reason to stop in and buy myself a sweet treat.

13

      I had car keys in hand and Anya ready to go when the doorbell rang.

"Sven and I are having a party here Saturday night," Leesa said, but she didn't act like she was a willing visitor. Instead, she stood on my front step at a distance.

Around her shoulders she wore an ice blue shawl that brought out the color of her eyes and a blue turtleneck that matched the wrap. Her hair was twisted into a knot on top of her head.

By contrast, I had pulled on a tired pair of maternity pants and one of George's sweatshirts from his college days. The "N" in Nike had rubbed off, leaving me to proudly proclaim, "ike."

Actually, it looked more like "Yikes!" because the minute I had picked her up, Anya had spit up pumpkin baby food all over me.

Goody! An invitation. They're finally coming around. For a split second, hope raised its lovely head, only to have its brains beaten out.

"Your workers put dirt and mud on our street. I do not want our guests to get that on their shoes. Your dirt will stain my carpet. You have to fix this right now." This was accompanied by a sweep of her right arm to indicate the vast mud pool we call "our lawn."

She finished with a sniff of disapproval and the demand, "You must do this." The look of blasé expectation on her face was priceless. Our neighborhood Nordic princess obviously believed that her wish was my command.

"Hmmm," I said. "How about if I rent one of those street-cleaning machines. You could drive it up and down until your heart's content. That way you'll be sure the pavement is fixed to your satisfaction."

"That might work if you drive it." She obviously did not understand sarcasm. "Also, you must to clean your sidewalk."

"Really? I must to clean it?"

"Yes. My friends will park in front of your house. It is only right. You do this for me."

"Do you need me to shine your shoes? Are your toilets clean? Should I wipe your butt?"

"I have cleaning lady for that. She take care of toilets and windows. I ask about butts. You fix street and sidewalk."

"I fix street and sidewalk," I repeated. "Roger Wilco. I'll hop right on it."

"No hopping. No Roger. No Wilco. You do this. You owe me."

"Um..." I pantomimed thinking this over. "I've decided. I owe you nothing. Not even the time of day. I think we're done here."

"Yes." She sneered. "Yes, absolutely."

14

_a_fter slamming the door and locking Leesa out of my house, I went back to my originally scheduled plan of action. First on my list was a trip to Kaldi's, that marvelous coffee vendor. As I pulled out of the garage, I waved to Leesa, but I only used one finger to bid her goodbye. My index finger. I was not going to teach my daughter a bad habit. No way!

The baristas at Kaldi's are not only friendly and efficient, but many of them have won competitions for creating images in coffee froth. How's that for an unusual artistic medium? Trying to guess what I'll see in my cup is always a highlight of my visits to Kaldi's. It's sort of like reading tea leaves. Somehow, the servers seem to have a sixth sense about what sort of message I need.

Today, either because of my rotten mood or the fact that Halloween displays were popping up, the barista duplicated Edvard Munch's famous painting, The Scream. Sure, the drawing matched my mood, but that was hardly the point. I took one look at my mug and burst into tears.

"Ma'am? I am so sorry. Are you okay?"

That led to me babbling about not being invited to a party.

All the servers gathered behind the counter to listen to my tale of woe. A girl with a long braid and a pierced nose shook her head in solidarity. "I hate mean girls. Sounds like you live next door to one of them."

"Across the street," I blubbered. "Mean girl lives across the street."

"Mama," said Anya, patting my cheek. "Mama sad."

"Here," said the manager, "I think this might cheer you up." She ducked behind the bakery case and retrieved a giant sugar cookie decorated with a female Frankenstein. "It's on the house."

There are very few problems in life that can't be solved with a big dose of sugar. Trust me on this.

Holding my precious cookie in one hand and my darling daughter by the other, I found a booth. The server brought me a new coffee with a smiley face in the froth. For Anya, there was a carton of milk. She and I had fun nibbling away at the green-faced monster on my cookie. I named body parts — eyes, ears, nose, mouth — as we bit down on them.

The sugar rush felt great. So good, in fact, that I wanted it to keep going. With Anya by my side, I walked over to the pastry case and said, "I loved that cookie, and I'd like to buy a dozen more."

Anya and I had great fun choosing ghosts, black cats, a haunted house, striped witch shoes, and other holiday icons. The manager gave me a discount. "You're a good customer, and it's the end of the day. Enjoy."

Feeling like I'd won the lottery, I remembered my initial reason for visiting. With the box of cookies in a paper bag, Anya and I perused the community bulletin board.

Two cleaning services caught my eye. Both looked like they were run by a single proprietor. Each offered tear-off tabs that made grabbing their phone numbers easy to do.

Yes, I'd been rejected by Leesa. But did I really want to attend a party at the Nordstroms' house?

No, I didn't.

What I really wanted — and needed — were friends of my own. People who would like and accept me for myself.

Once I got my house in order, I would set about finding them.

15

*A*fter we got home, I dialed the number on the first slip of paper from Kaldi's.

"Yell-ow," answered a voice at the other end.

I do not understand why saying "yellow" instead of "hello" strikes people as funny. To me, it sounds like nails on a chalkboard. Trés hillbilly.

"Hi, my name is Kiki Lowenstein. I'm looking for a cleaning lady."

"You found her. When can I start?"

That wasn't exactly what I'd expected. In my head, I was the one who'd make the decision whether to hire the person on the other end of the line.

"Yes, well, I thought you'd like to hear about my needs."

The woman chuckled. "Let me guess. You want clean toilets. Vacuuming. Mopping floors. Ain't that what cleaning's all about? Not too different from house to house."

Except most houses weren't as messy as mine. Clearly, this nice woman didn't understand the full extent of my problem. I decided to get down to the nitty-gritty. "Right, except this is new construction. We moved in the same day the builders moved out."

"Sawdust all over the place? That's what you're saying?"

"Exactly." I smiled. We were making progress.

"I can't help you. I'm allergic to sawdust." With that, she hung up the phone.

Onward and upward. I dialed the second number.

"Yes?"

"I'm calling about a cleaning lady?"

"Yes. I clean houses. How big is yours?"

"Nearly four thousand square feet."

Silence.

"Ma'am?" I prodded. "Are you there?"

"Lady, that ain't no house. That's a barn. It's too much for me. Good luck."

After my second hang-up in a row, I turned my attention to the serious business of eating iced cookies.

16

Two days later, and I was willing to call it quits. No one seemed willing or interested or available to clean my house.

Meanwhile, the Nordstroms' party preparations shifted into high gear. While I watched, their cleaning lady bustled around, flitting from one job to the next. She hauled an extension ladder out of her Toyota truck and propped it against their outside walls. After climbing the ladder, she washed the second floor windows, using a squeegee to get them streak-free.

Next, she tackled the first floor windows, and these were dirtier by far. This worker bee buzzed right through the job. As she attacked the glass with gusto, her multitude of earrings sparkled in the sunlight. The excessive jewelry seemed rather at odds to her pared down uniform of white polo shirt, black slacks, and black tennis shoes.

After finishing the windows in what seemed like record time, she put the ladder away and disappeared inside the Nordstrom home.

Why couldn't I find a person as industrious as the woman cleaning my neighbors' house? Life can be so unfair.

A bit later, a florist truck pulled up. Two men delivered bouquets of all sizes.

Not long after the flower boys left, a catering truck took its place in the Nordstroms' drive. The crew members were dressed in crisp white shirts, black vests, and black pants. Like a stream of hard-working ants, they toted silver serving trays into the house. Watching all this pre-party preparation caused an emotional throw-back to fourth grade. Every girl in my class had been invited to Cricket Henderson's birthday party. Every girl, that is, but me. When asked about the exclusion by our teacher, Cricket claimed that she had found one of my curls in her sandwich. I had begun my career as a social outcast at the tender age of nine.

Old hurts run deep. They hide inside you, only to be awakened at a moment's notice. Tearing myself away from the scene outside my window, I tried not to pay attention to the preparations underway at the Nordstroms' place. But even without watching all of the activity, I felt hurt.

At five thirty, George phoned to say he had a late meeting and would be spending the night at his mother's house. "It's closer."

Right. By five minutes. Maybe. That was the capper to my very bad, awful, horrible, no-good day. I burst into tears while changing Anya's diaper.

Toilet-training. The next horizon. Was I up to the task?

Nope. Not right now. It presented yet another challenge, another way for me to live in squalor.

I'd just made it downstairs with Anya when Leesa rang the doorbell. She looked like a hooker who had decided to go door to door and collect for charity. My mean girl neighbor was wearing a scarlet red dress, cut low in the bodice and high on the thigh.

"Yes?" I stared into Leesa's glamorous face. She'd gone all out with artfully applied mascara, liner, and blush.

"There is no room in our driveway. Our caterer must park in yours. That is best. You never go out in evenings anyway."

My lower lip trembled, but I was not about to cry in front of her. In my mind, I penned a letter to Miss Manners, who would certainly label Leesa as a rude pig.

Struggling to tamp down my emotions, I realized this might be my chance to repair a bit of the damage I'd done earlier by losing my temper. What difference did it make where the caterers parked their van? George wasn't coming home. Leesa was quite correct: I wasn't going out. Maybe I could earn a few brownie points with the Ice Goddess.

"Sure. No problem."

17

By eight o'clock, the Nordstroms' party was in full swing. Not only had the caterer parked in our driveway, but another car, a black Jaguar, had pulled up as well. It now blocked the catering van. I noticed all this from my second floor, where I rocked Anya in the wooden rocking chair, until she fell asleep in my arms.

Reluctant to sleep alone in my big, empty marital bed, I crawled into the twin bed opposite her crib. For hours, I listened to the slamming of car doors. Intoxicated laughter and chatter drifted into Anya's room.

Around midnight, Anya rustled around in her bed. Tiny catlike noises signaled she was dreaming.

Since becoming a mom, I'm hyper-sensitive to sounds. Although I could have rolled over and gone to sleep, I got up and checked on her.

She'd scooted to one end of her crib and positioned herself awkwardly. Gently, I rearranged her. Once settled, she sighed with contentment and snored lightly.

Of course, I had to tinkle. I always do when I wake up in the night. Because I use the bathroom frequently, I didn't need to turn on the light. I am an expert at making my way in the dark.

When I finished, I heard loud voices from the Nordstroms' deck. After washing my hands, I pried open the bathroom window and peeked between the blinds.

Leesa's wheat-colored hair caught the light from one end of their portico. Her bob gleamed like a Viking helmet in the velvet darkness. Another face came into focus. This woman was shorter than Leesa, with a curvy build. As she stepped into the circle of illumination, her copper-red hair glowed with the intensity of an ember.

Both women gestured wildly. Their voices traveled through the night in a shrill point and counterpoint that occasionally overlapped, the way any argument does. Although their faces were hidden by the structure of the porch with its narrow roof, their emotions came across clearly. As I watched, they advanced on each other, until the personal space between them disappeared.

The quarrel stopped, when a third woman stepped out of the front door. I could only see her legs as she hesitated on the threshold. Leesa and the redhead turned their attention to the newcomer. Voices still rode the night air, but now their timbre had softened.

Or so it seemed.

With a screech, one of the women cursed. I couldn't make out the exact sentiment, but it caused Leesa to stamp her foot. Again, the voices crescendoed, growing louder and angrier.

Just when I thought a cat fight would ensue, the front door opened yet again. Sven stepped into the fray. Like a kindly good shepherd, he herded the three women back into his house.

18

*A*round two, loud voices woke me from an uneasy slumber. First, I rolled over, pulled the pillow over my head, and tried to shut them out. But I couldn't. Finally, I walked to the window.

The argument was taking place in our driveway. Leesa, Sven, and another man spoke a foreign tongue in loud voices, punctuated by aggressive gestures. Around and around they went, their voices climbing higher and higher, in what I assumed was Swedish or Finnish or whatever they spoke in the frozen land of their ancestors.

Suddenly there came a sudden bellow of anger, as Sven pushed the stranger backwards, slamming him hard against the bumper of the black Jaguar. Almost immediately, catering staff arrived on the scene. They lined up behind the quarrelsome trio. The shiny surfaces of pans and trays caught the light from our street lamp and reflected it in eerie flashes, reminiscent of lightning.

The Jaguar's owner shoved Sven backwards. As my neighbor fought to regain his balance, Jaguar Man climbed into his car.

Before backing out, he revved the powerful motor. With a squeal, he peeled rubber, spinning his wheels as he reversed out of the driveway. The smell of hot rubber drifted up to my open window.

With the sports car out of the way, the caterers streamed around Leesa and Sven in a single file, not breaking stride, moving ever forward toward their goal. I counted six members of the serving staff. In the dark silence of the night, the Nordstroms huddled together and bent their heads to confer. For a short while, it seemed the conflict was over. Whatever words had passed among the three of them would be forgotten.

Four of the hired help headed back into the Nordstroms' house. Two members of the catering staff worked to secure the items inside the truck. I rocked back on my heels, in preparation to leave. But before I could drop the slats, I heard a stinging slap. Sven's head snapped backward. After staggering to one side, he began massaging his jaw. Leesa moved into his personal space. He grabbed her by the wrists. The roar from his throat sounded like it came from a lion at the St. Louis Zoo. She fought his grip and sputtered what I assume were curses.

I'd seen and heard enough. The Nordstroms' quarrel brought back bad memories from my childhood. Creeping away from the window, I crawled into the single bed and pulled the covers over my face. Eventually, I must have dozed off. I spent the rest of the night tossing and turning fitfully. At some point, Anya muttered in her sleep. Thinking she might need comfort, I got out of bed and stood over her crib to stroke her hair.

What dreams did my daughter have?

I prayed they were sweet ones. With any luck, she wouldn't realize the tension between her father and me. From the git-go, George had been adamant about wanting a child — and, therefore, insisting that we get married.

But he had never said he loved me. Not even once. More and more frequently, he didn't return home at night. His excuses varied, but the shame-faced way he explained his decision had grown increasingly familiar.

Maybe he regretted his decision for us to become a family.

I hoped not.

19

The next morning, Anya and I were up early. As was our routine, after getting her dressed, we held hands and stepped outside to pick up the newspaper. We had made it to the end of the driveway, when Sven whizzed past us on his expensive racing bike.

George hadn't come home until the wee hours of the morning. I heard him as he crept up the stairs and into the guest bedroom. That struck me as odd, since he'd said he was staying at Sheila's. Of course I knew the reason why: He had lied to me. Idly, I wondered what it might feel like to slap him the way that Leesa had smacked Sven.

But I would never do that in front of Anya. Ever. Instead, I carried on like the dutiful mother and wife I was.

I was picking up the Cheerios that were strewn around our kitchen like confetti, when the crunch of his shoes alerted me to his presence.

"Good morning," George said. "I see somebody has thrown me a parade!"

My daughter gurgled with delight at the sight of her dad. His bloodshot eyes didn't bother her one bit. As usual, he picked her up and gave her a cuddle, a familiar gesture that provoked an ache in my heart. Why couldn't he show me more affection?

Well, duh. Obviously because he was getting it from some- where — correction, *someone* — else.

"I thought you were staying overnight at your mother's." I tried to sound casual.

"That was the plan, but she withdrew her invitation." He couldn't meet my gaze. "What's new with you?"

"Not much." I told him about the Nordstroms' party, and on a whim, mentioned the fight I'd seen in the driveway. Watching George's face carefully, I added, "It was a confrontation of sorts. Pretty ugly."

"Hmm." George kept his back to me and busied himself making a new pot of coffee. "Let's hope it blows over. They do seem ideally suited to each other. Same values and all that. Hobbies. Like how they go bike-riding. That reminds me. I think you might enjoy golf. I know you love nature, and there's that saying about how golf is a good walk spoiled. I signed you up for private lessons at the club. If you find you enjoy the game, it might be fun. We could do it together."

A lump forced in my throat.

Bless him, he was trying.

"Sure," I said. "If I can find a sitter."

"Taken care of. Mom will call you later today."

20

Shortly after George left, Sheila phoned me. "Your first golf lesson is at ten. I'll be over in fifteen minutes to babysit Anya."

"Okay." Expecting Sheila to be gracious was like asking a tiger to take small bites while eating. I decided to make the best of the situation. "Anya will be thrilled to see you."

"And I her." With that, my mother-in-law hung up the phone.

Putting my daughter in her playpen, I spent the next ten minutes doing my best to pick up the house. It wasn't easy. Moving boxes cluttered most of the rooms, making it impossible to run a vacuum. Sawdust had piled up on every horizontal surface. The floors and baseboards needed a good scrubbing. By shoving as much as I could in the closets, I did manage to tidy up. My goal of passing Sheila's inspection kept me hopping until the doorbell rang. By the time I answered it, I was damp with sweat, and my hair had escaped its scrunchie to fly around my face.

By contrast, Sheila looked like she had just stepped out of a bandbox, as my nana would have put it. (Although admittedly, while I don't understand why this metaphor makes sense, it sounds plausible.) Her silver-white hair perfectly framed her face and contrasted nicely with the huge designer sunglasses she always wore. Her tan gabardine slacks hung perfectly from her slender hips. The pants were topped with a nubby knit ivory sweater. Around her shoulders was a pashmina in glorious fall colors.

"Hi, Sheila, how are you?" I ushered her in, ignoring the less than joyful expression on her face. I knew it would change when she clapped eyes on Anya — and it did.

My mother-in-law walked right past me, straight to her grandchild, and scooped up Anya in her arms. "Darling girl! How are you? Beautiful as ever, I see. Aren't you adorable?"

Smooches ensued. I picked up my purse. The sound of my rattling keys caused Sheila to whirl around.

"Kiki, you are not wearing that to the golf club, are you?"

I looked down at myself. I was wearing my best jeans, a pink cotton turtleneck sweater, and a jacket. "Um, yeah."

"You cannot wear denim into the club. It is not allowed. Really. I thought you knew better."

I raced upstairs to change into a worn pair of black knit slacks. Once properly attired, I hoped to scoot past Sheila and out the front door, but Old Eagle Eyes waited to give me a once-over. "That's not strictly appropriate; however, it will suffice I guess. While you are at the club, take the opportunity to look around at what other women are wearing and adjust your wardrobe accordingly. If all goes well, you will meet suitable people on the course and begin to make friends."

"Friends?" I repeated the word, because I didn't know that she or her son had noticed how lonely I was.

"Yes. Friends. Role models. People in our social circle. Other mothers who can guide you as Anya grows."

"I'd like that."

21

My golf career was blessedly short. It lasted all of one class.

"Hit that tiny ball? Really?" I shook my head as I studied the object on the tee. "And I'm supposed to put it over where?"

"There." Rod Oberman pointed at a spot way, way off in the distance.

"Why?" I squinted in the sunlight. "I mean, why is it so far? How do I guide the ball?"

"The way you hit it will determine the flight path."

"Right. If I hit it. I'm, uh, not good with balls. In college, I got smacked in the face by a softball, volleyball, and tennis ball all in one class."

Rod inhaled and let it out slowly. My teacher — the club's golf pro — was a pretty boy, muscular but slender. As he strode around the clubhouse, folks kept stopping him to chat. By my assessment, he'd wasted at least a half an hour of our class time as he glad-handed his admirers.

I also noticed he didn't bother to introduce me. Nana would have tut-tutted his lack of good manners. Personally, I was more annoyed at how he acted like he'd been forced to play nurse-maid to a sub-human creature.

My husband and mother-in-law were paying him to encourage me to take up a new hobby. Instead, this creep was doing everything he could to make me feel uncomfortable and awkward. I swore right then and there that, if I ever had the chance to teach other people a skill, I'd do my best to make them feel good about themselves — even if they never learned a thing, they would leave feeling upbeat.

"You were hit in the face?" His question was rhetorical. "You're in luck. This time, you're launching the balls. There's no chance you're going to get hit. Even if you forget to duck. Only a moron would get hit with a golf ball."

That sounded more like a challenge rather than a reassurance. Okay, two could play this game.

"So, the ball goes over by the flag, right? But I can barely see that flag. You're sure there's a hole over there? On the other side of that hill?"

"Just aim it at the flag. We'll worry about getting it inside a hole later."

I shrugged. "Okey-dokey."

I missed the ball five times in a row. In fact, my club and the ball never did meet in passing. "I don't think this is the game for me. It just doesn't feel like a good fit."

"You don't know much about golf, do you? When you know more, you'll love it." Rod's mouth twisted into a painful imitation of a polite smile. "George told me you like nature. When you see how wonderful the grounds are, you'll fall in love with the sport. How about if we take a tour of the course? Maybe that will calm you down, and you'll see why people get addicted to golf."

That sounded like a grand idea, and Rod's voice was friendlier than it had been. However, when I wanted to stop and pick up a bird's nest that had fallen to the ground, he was not happy.

"There could be bugs on that."

"I'll put it in a garbage bag and spray it with bug killer, when I get home."

"But, in the meantime, they could crawl around in the golf cart and get on us."

"Nah. Not likely," I said. "That would be a long, long hike for itsy-bitsy bugs."

I wanted to add, "Boy, are you a wuss." But I didn't. Instead, seeing the look of panic on his face, I gave in and left the bird nest on the ground.

"Can I drive the golf cart?" I asked.

"I think it's best that I do the driving," he said smugly. That annoyed me, because I thought zooming around in that little doo-jobbie would be fun.

"Stop!" I yelled, as we came over a crest. "Look at that! Over there!"

"What?"

"Wow. I've never seen a daisy that small. It's, like, dollhouse size. Drive over there, please." I stood up to see the flower better.

"Not a good idea," Rod said. "It's just off the fairway. We could get hit."

"Wait a minute. You said that only morons get hit."

That's when a golf ball smacked him in the eye.

But I have to give it to him. He was right. Only morons get hit with golf balls.

That night, I overheard George talking to his mother on the phone. "Rod's lucky he didn't lose an eye. They're telling me he'll survive. I guess Kiki will never be a golfer. Hey, it's okay. Saves me money on club fees, equipment, and clothes."

22

*S*ince golfing wasn't my cup of tea, I redoubled my efforts to whip the house into shape. The next day while I washed dishes by hand, I hatched a plan. First, I would tackle getting all our boxes unpacked. We'd moved to this house from a small apartment, and really there weren't all that many containers. But they were bulky and big. Right after George left for work, I put Anya in her playpen. I figured I'd tackle the boxes one by one. Getting them emptied, broken down, and moved out of the open space would go a long way toward making our new house a home.

Two hours later, my muscles ached from lugging the boxes around. I'd opened four, all with kitchen items inside. Rather than put these directly into the cabinets, I figured they could do with a good wash.

While I finished up, Anya grew more and more fussy. I couldn't blame her. She'd been in her playpen for a long time. The walls felt like they were closing in on me. What we needed was a nice ride in the car, the old BMW convertible that George had impulsively purchased.

Where to go? The pots and pans had left black marks on our

white enamel sink. I had tackled them with Comet, but they still thumbed their noses at me.

"Home Depot, Anya. What do you think? We could even pick up a few pots of mums while we're there."

I was backing out of our garage, when Sven Nordstrom careened behind me on his bicycle. While I waited for him to pass, he slammed his bike into the curb. The abrupt stop threw him over his handlebars and onto the grass. As a final punctuation to the metallic clatter, there came the hollow sound of an empty Gatorade bottle rolling into the gutter.

"Anya, I'll be right back." Turning off the car and leaving the door open, I ran to see if Sven was badly hurt.

"Mr. Nordstrom?" I circled around his prone figure, trying to get a good look at his face. He was staring straight ahead, and he seemed stunned.

"It's me, Kiki. Your neighbor. Can you get up?" To my surprise, he didn't try to extricate himself from the tangle of metal tubes and wheels. "Sven? Are you all right? Should I call someone?"

"Help." His voice was weak.

I dialed 911, raced back to my car to check on Anya, hoisted her onto my hip, jogged back to where Sven was, and waited for help to arrive. And it did, quickly. After flagging down the EMTs and offering up what few details I had, Anya and I retreated to an out of the way vantage spot across the street.

"Ride?" Anya chirped and pointed at my waiting BMW. Although she fought the restraints of the car seat, she dearly loved any trip by automobile.

"Not yet, sweetheart." I bounced her on my hip in an attempt to quell her restlessness.

"Ride!" she demanded.

"In a minute, honey."

As the ambulance pulled away from the curb, I spotted the

empty Gatorade bottle that had rolled away from Sven Nordstrom's bike. The plastic container nagged at me, as it lolled there in the gutter.

George and I are both big into recycling. That bottle tickled my conscience. We agreed that people who toss trash into the environment should be fined. Once, when following a litterbug, George had hopped out of the car and returned an empty soda can to the guy who'd thrown it on the road. I'd sat there, shaking with fear, since Missouri is a concealed carry state.

"Ride!" Anya's voice grew ever more insistent.

But the empty bottle nagged my conscience. Crossing the street one more time, I reached down and swooped up the Gatorade container.

"Ride, ride, ride!" Anya screeched in my ear. Her patience had hit its limits.

I carried her directly to her car seat, where she shocked me by eagerly sinking into the contraption. After fussing with the various buckles and straps to keep Anya safe, I tossed the empty bottle into the footwell below her feet in the back seat. Finally, I climbed in and keyed the engine. I turned my head in time to see my contrary little miss grinning at me, her two new teeth gleaming in an adorable parody of a jack-o-lantern.

23

First I drove us to our local Home Depot. Having a task to keep me occupied seemed like a useful — even necessary — diversion. Worrying about Sven Nordstrom wasn't going to do anybody any good.

"Down. Down. Down!" Anya fought me as I tried to wrestle her into a shopping cart.

Her new favorite thing was to toddle along beside the cart, holding onto it for balance. George thought it the most precious trick ever. I disagreed. I worried, because she tended to pick up anything and everything she found that sparked her interest. She took after her mother, I guess. I've always been attracted to the idea of turning trash into treasure. I love crafts of any kind.

As Anya wobbled her way around the store, I kept a careful watch on my baby and on other shoppers. We took up nearly the whole width of an aisle. Other patrons in a hurry found us a cumbersome challenge.

But Anya was having a blast. Her newfound freedom brought a drooling smile to her face. Twice she shrieked with pleasure. I did my best to ignore any reactions other than those who clearly saw my child as the too-cute-for-words baby she was.

In the cleaning products aisle, I picked up Comet and read the label. Soft Scrub, too. I had used both on the sink, but the black marks hadn't budged. Was there a new and improved version of these old standbys? Or an unknown-to-me product that could really provide tons of oomph?

I waved to a guy wearing an orange vest and described my problem. Running a beefy hand over his big belly, he wagged his head. "Beats me, lady. Comet didn't take it out?"

Behind me, a woman cleared her throat.

"Am I in your way?" I reached for Anya's hand.

"No, you're fine. What you need is ZUD®." A pair of elaborately made-up eyes locked onto mine. How she could see anything through all that mascara was a mystery.

"ZUD?" I repeated slowly. At the edge of my peripheral vision, the man in orange backed away.

"The name's Mert. Mert Chambers."

"I'm Kiki. Kiki Lowenstein." I offered my hand for a shake, as I tried to place where I'd seen Mert before.

"Nice to meet you," she said, with a nod that sent her multitude of earrings swinging.

"You work on my neighbor's house. The Nordstroms' place, don't you?"

"Yes, ma'am. Been there for nearly two years. Got the job after they canned their old housecleaner. Are you the family that moved into the house cattywampus from theirs? Kinda, sorta across the street?"

"That's us. This is my daughter, Anya," I said. "I'm having a heck of a time getting the house in shape. You're saying that ZUD will work on stained white enamel? How do you know?"

"Because I take pride in being good at what I do. Now let me tell you how to fix your problem. Take home a can of this here

ZUD. Wet your enamel sink. Sprinkle this on. Let it sink in for ten minutes. Scrub it. Rinse. I bet that mark will disappear the first time you use this."

The words were no more than out of Mert's mouth, when Anya let out a terrified cry.

24

My daughter sobbed so hard that I couldn't tell what was wrong. Not at first. Only after I shifted her from my right hip to my left did I glimpse something bright orange inside her nose.

"What on earth?" I tilted Anya's head back for a better look. Mr. Orange Vest reappeared, probably to make sure I wasn't hurting my child.

"She stuck something up her nose," Mert said, after one quick look. "Wonder what?"

While I tried to calm Anya, Mert scanned the floor.

Sure enough, half hidden by a shelf unit, she found the torn top of an M&M's bag.

"I got it!" Mert brought the evidence to me.

Anya's panic mellowed into soft sobs.

Derrick, the guy in the orange vest, shook his head. "Well, I'll be jiggered. I ain't seen a kid do that in years. Not since my Donnie stuck a crayon up his nose."

Mert daintily covered her mouth and snickered. "My kid done put a Lego brick in his. Liked to never get that out."

"Shhh," I said, as I rocked Anya. "It's okay, honey. I'm going to pinch your nose like —"

But I never got to finish. She tossed back her head and screamed bloody murder. "Noooooo!"

I couldn't blame her. Having a nostril pinched shut was unpleasant in the best of times. Scary stuff.

"Emergency room here we come," I said, fighting Anya to put her into the kid's seat of the shopping cart.

"No way." Mert laughed. "We can get that there candy out in two shakes of a puppy dog tail. Ever' thing we need is right here.
"

I gulped. *Should I trust this woman?*

Then I thought about explaining this to George. What would he say when he learned I wasn't watching our child more closely? Wasn't vigilance Job One?

"You really think you can get it out?"

"I know I can. But I'm gonna need a little help from this nice hunk. Derrick, hon? You got a shop vac? There's one hooked up over by the saw, ain't it? Can you grab me a roll of duct tape?"

Mr. Orange Vest nodded eagerly. Being called "a hunk" had cause him to perk up like a plant thirsty for water. "The shop vac is right this way. You follow me. I'll grab the duct tape while we're walking."

Anya continued to boo-hoo, but the confident attitude of our new friends intrigued her. Mert slipped off a bracelet and gave it to my daughter to play with. Since Mert was wearing ten on one arm, the loss didn't detract from her look at all. While we strolled to the shop vac, I noticed she collected once-overs from admiring men.

"Shop vac?" I repeated. "That makes me feel faintly queasy. You aren't going to, uh, suck that candy out of her, are you?"

Mert put a finger to her lip. Anya busily tried on the bracelet and clanged it against the metal handle of the cart.

"Hush. It'll be all right. You'll see. I won't do nothing without your permission."

That was mildly comforting.

Derrick signaled for us to stop at Aisle 15. He raced away and returned with a roll of silver duct tape.

"Perfect." With a wink, Mert pulled a Bic pen from the plastic pocket protector in his shirt pocket. As her fingers brushed the fabric, I could see the man thrill to her touch. My face must have been as red as his vest was orange.

"You don't mind if I take this here pen apart, do you?" Mert batted thick lashes at him. "You're such a gallant gentleman that I don't wanna take no advantage of you."

"At your service!" Derrick clicked his heels in a mock salute, although the scuffed tennis shoes didn't make a sound.

After parading a few yards farther along the center of the store, we arrived at the circular saw used to cut lumber for patrons. Anya's eyes widened in terror. She opened her mouth to scream, but Mert handed over yet another bracelet.

Thus mollified, my child played happily, while Derrick scrambled under the table, burrowed through sawdust, and yanked free one end of a shop vac tube.

Crushing the tip of the pen under the heel of her boot, Mert pulled out the ballpoint and spring. All that remained was the white tube. After tearing the cellophane off the duct tape, she wrapped the silver adhesive strip around the pen and the open end of the vacuum hose. A couple of deft twirls later, the nozzle had been reduced from an aperture of maybe 2" wide to the smaller tube of the ink pen.

Leaning close to me, Mert spoke in a low voice. "I'm gonna touch this here small tube to the M&M and suck it out. To make sure I don't hurt her none, I'll grip the pen right down here at the opening. That way I can control it to suction better."

Straightening, she gave me an even look. "Of course, I ain't gonna do nothing unless you're comfortable with it. If you decide you'd rather visit the hospital, that's good by me."

Derrick stood off to one side, his eyes darting from Mert's cleavage to Anya's flushed face.

I took the empty pen casing from Mert's hand. Given how small the tube was, I couldn't see any way it would hurt Anya.

"Do it," I said.

25

I was cradling Anya in my arms, as I shifted my weight from one foot to the other. She still sniffled, but mainly, she was totally fascinated by all the industry around her. Anya's eyes followed every move made by the three of us adults. Her lower lip trembled with fear.

I kissed her wet cheek. "It's okay, sweetie. We're going to help you breathe. I know that your nose hurts."

As I soothed my daughter, Mert wisely held the tube behind her back, the way my dentist always blocks the sight of his hypodermic needle. Derrick stood slightly behind Mert, filling the aisle and fending off other customers. We were seriously blocking traffic, but the operation was too delicate to leave to chance. What if somebody bumped Mert's elbow as she pointed that tube at my daughter's face?

"Hey, buttercup," Mert cooed to Anya. "You want another one of my bracelets?"

After pulling off Gold Cuff #3, Mert handed it to my daughter. Anya solemnly added it to the pair already on her arm. The distraction kept my child from screaming her head off.

As Mert advanced on her, Anya turned her face toward me.

But I gripped her chin tightly, while Mert swooped down with the tube. Those blue eyes blinked up at me in shock — I could read the question, *What are you doing, Mama?* — but Mert was fully prepared. More importantly, she moved fast. In a flash, the white tube swooped down toward the target. The tip of the tube disappeared inside Anya's nostril, right as my daughter opened her mouth to let go a startled cry.

But in less than a second, the problem was solved. With a slurp, the vacuum sucked up the M&M candy. It stuck to the end of the ink pen tube, a trophy if I'd ever seen one.

"Ta-dah!" Mert held up the prize for inspection.

"Tan-dy" Anya grabbed for it.

"No way, kiddo. It'll be a cold day in August when I let you near another M&M. Maybe about the time you're seventeen or so."

Mert snickered. Handing the nozzle to Derrick, she thanked him for his help.

"I was thinking you might like to go out or something and grab a beer with me." He pinked up as he issued this invitation, his complexion contrasting brightly with the orange vest. "But I'm gonna need your phone number, if you're willing to make concrete plans."

"Here's my card." Mert wiggled her fingers inside her back pocket. Producing two business cards, she gave one to Derrick and one to me.

On the left was a silhouette of a woman pushing a vacuum cleaner. To the right, a jaunty slogan, "Got dirt? Get Mert," soared directly above her name and phone number.

"Well, I've got dirt," I said. "Lots and lots of it. In fact, my kitchen sink is the least of my problems. We moved into our house right as the construction workers packed up and left. You wouldn't believe what a mess I have on my hands."

"Oh, yes, I would. I get lots of calls to do new construction cleaning. Don't forget; I've seen that place of yours. You need lots of help. That place is huge. I'm the one who can get it spruced up for you. Shoot, I got a vacuum cleaner that can suck up a bowling ball. I'll get you fixed up in no time."

She didn't have her calendar with her, so I promised I would call her that very evening.

"Anya? We need to give those bracelets back to Mert." My daughter had quit crying and gotten down to the serious work of slipping the bracelets up and down on her tiny arms.

"No!" The cherubic face turned mulish.

Mert smiled at me and at my daughter. "I'll get 'em when I come to clean. There isn't a girl on earth who'd willingly give up her bangles. No reason to fight her for them. Especially after she's had such a rough morning already."

Amen to that.

26

_M_ert and I went our separate ways. She was on a cleaning supply run, which took her to the left; I guided our shopping cart to the garden area, off to the right. There, a glorious selection of seasonal flowers begged to come home with us.

"Flo-ow-ees!" Anya clapped her tiny hands with joy.

The display sent my senses into overdrive. Vibrant maroon, bright yellow, and robust orange blossoms competed with each other for attention as they sat on top of a bale of hay. Forming a ring around the bale was a lineup of asters in various shades of purple. Pumpkins of all sizes flanked the flowers, while multi-colored bunches of Indian corn were hung from peg board to create a patterned backdrop.

I went a wee bit nuts. First, I buried my nose in a gathering of spicy blossoms. After I'd had a good sniff, I loaded our cart with as many mums and asters as it would hold.

We might not have grass, but we sure as shooting were going to have lots and lots of flowers. I couldn't wait to see how they perked up the sea of brown mud that framed our house.

Once all my prizes were safely jam-packed into my car, I hit the button and lowered the top. There wouldn't be many more beautiful days like this. Why shouldn't Anya and I enjoy the fresh air? Rather than going straight home, I decided we should stop at McDonald's. Anya had been carefully trained by me to scream with joy whenever she saw those golden arches.

As we approached the drive-up window, she chanted, "Appy-eel. Appy-eel."

"Yes, Mama will get you a Happy Meal." When the squawk box greeted us, I placed an order for my fish filet and her Happy Meal.

"Boy or girl?" asked the disembodied voice.

The word "girl" was on the tip of my tongue, until I noticed that the boys' toys were much cooler than the girls' selection. "Boy," I said.

At the window, a cute young man in a server's uniform did a double-take, when he saw Anya sitting in her car seat. Her cute orange bow had drifted to just above her left ear. "Just a minute, ma'am. We've got you the wrong toy."

"I asked for a boy toy." Instantly, I blushed. "I mean, I want a toy for a boy."

"But you have a little girl."

"Yes, but your girl toys are boring. Come on, buddy. Who wants a Miss Kitty statue? But a plastic bug? That's totally cool."

Sticking his head all the way out of the window, he said, "Hey, I'm with you, lady. Just wanted to make sure you knew what you were getting. Most moms would go bananas if we didn't hand over the gender appropriate toy. You'd be amazed. Give me a sec, and I'll grab a plastic bug. Or two."

He returned with a Happy Meal box and an iconic white paper bag printed with those golden arches. "Be careful. I just handed you a bag full of bugs." He grinned and added, "Considering you've got a car full of plants. They'll probably fit right in."

Giggling, I thanked him and pulled into a parking space. I

tore Anya's burger into smaller pieces while I ate my fish sand-wich. She munched on fries, and I enjoyed my ice tea. When we'd eaten our fill, I tossed out the garbage. I'd left the bag of bugs for last, but now I opened it up to find plastic models of a locust, a fly, a centipede, and a spider. Ripping off the packaging, I handed Anya the centipede. The toy earned a loud crow of approval.

Pushing her favorite tape into the cassette player, I listened for the cheerful sounds of Anya's favorite song, *The Wheels on the Bus.*

The other bugs went into the glove compartment to save for a rainy day. While Anya examined her centipede with the sort of concentration only a toddler can have, I pulled out of the parking space and headed for home. Overhead, the turning leaves formed a canopy of autumnal shades. A light breeze lifted my curls. Anya talked up a storm to the bug, probably explaining exactly why she'd decided to poke an M&M up into her nose.

All was right with my world, until I paused at a four-way stop sign and a squirrel fell into my car.

27

*L*anding with a *thunk* on the console, the furry critter was as shocked as I was. Those tiny brown eyes locked onto mine, and I swear he let out a gasp as he stared up at me.

I shrieked.

His little mouth quivered.

We were both scared out of our minds.

From the back seat, Anya had watched the drop. At first, she was stunned, too. Then she yelled, "Quirrel! Quirrel!" and fought to climb out of her car seat. Fortunately, even I have trouble latching and unlatching all those straps that keep her secure. Otherwise, she would have scrambled from the back seat to the front in a flash.

I don't know how I had the presence of mind, but I managed to shove the gear shift into park. Otherwise the BMW would have rolled into the intersection. Because I couldn't run off and leave my baby, I could only huddle against my side of the car. The squirrel shook his tiny head, trying to work out what had just happened.

"Help! Eeek!" I screamed. It was an involuntary response. I didn't expect anyone to come to our aid.

The disoriented rodent chattered. His tiny teeth clacked. His bushy tail twitched in annoyance. Taking two steps, he wobbled like a drunken sailor. He grabbed at the dash and tried to climb it. He succeeded cranking up the volume of the tape to a roar.

"Round and round!" shrieked the chorus.

Of course, the squirrel couldn't get a purchase on the slick knobs and buttons. About halfway up, he toppled over backward. After bonking into the stick shift, he tumbled sideways into the passenger seat and landed in a pot of mums. Using his miniscule toenails, he shredded the maroon blossoms into confetti.

"Leave my flowers alone!" I yelled, over the singing from the cassette tape. "Get out!"

Out of nowhere, a man appeared at my side. "Lady? You okay?"

"Squirrel!" I pointed. The song on the tape switched, and a woman sang loudly, "The farmer in the dell, the farmer in the dell."

The moment was surreal. I quickly cranked down the volume, while the furry intruder tried to dig his way into the pot of mums.

"A what?" The man asked. One hand smoothed his tie to keep it from dragging against my dirty car. With his nice suit and white shirt, he belonged behind a desk in a bank, not in the middle of a Ladue side street.

I cranked down the volume, but "farmer takes a pig" still came through loud and clear.

"There's a squirrel in my car! I have to get him out! What if he bites my daughter?"

My would-be rescuer followed the direction of my finger. A

fuzzy gray head popped up in the pot of mums. "Whoa! What the heck?"

Confronted by two humans, my unwilling passenger panicked. He decided to scramble up the back of the seat. His tiny claws sank into the leather, but only barely. His little legs were moving double-time, like a hamster on a treadmill.

"Get away from my daughter!" I yelled, and, with a quick brush of my hand, I swept the rodent off the headrest.

He landed in the mums again.

"I'll get him." The man raced around to the passenger side of the BMW. As he jogged, his tie bobbed up and down. But, once he rounded the bumper and came face-to-face with the squirrel, my rescuer froze. It finally dawned on him he'd have to grab the squirrel with his bare hands.

Meanwhile, the squirrel was getting his wits about him. He glanced around and realized freedom was overhead. With a mighty leap, he threw himself at my passenger door. Seeing the furry fuzzball race toward him, Mr. Businessman backed away from the car.

I took action.

I pressed the button that rolled down the side window. Recalculating the wind speed, distance, and necessary velocity, the squirrel lunged forward once again. Using his back legs as a springboard, the squirrel managed to heave himself up and over the passenger side of my car.

As my rescuer, Anya, and I watched, the squirrel streaked across the street, and raced up a nearby tree.

28

*N*ever had one child experienced so much excitement in a morning.

Anya begged the squirrel to come back, but thankfully, the rat-with-a-fluffy-tail was not interested in exploring our car further. After making sure that Anya and I were unharmed, Mr. Businessman climbed back in his car. I figured he'd be telling his story to his office co-workers for years to come. It would be the stuff of legends.

The mums in my passenger seat looked like they'd been caught up in a weed whacker. More importantly, Anya was safe. So was I. No squirrels had been harmed in the making of this memory. Also my car was still drivable, which would not have been the case if we'd tangled with one of the many deer that lived in the St. Louis area.

Although I shook like one of the leaves in the maple trees overhead, I got us home in one piece.

Experience is a cruel, but effective, teacher. As I pulled into our garage, I thought about going next door and asking after Sven. I worried about that feeble cry for help he'd made. His bike was still resting on its side, there in the Nordstroms' yard.

But why invite trouble? If Sven was fine — and I figured he was — then he wouldn't want me to make a fuss about his tumble. If he was ailing, Leesa would answer the door, and that would mean a close encounter of the negative kind.

I didn't see any signs of life at the house across the street. Maybe I should leave well enough alone. I'd certainly had enough excitement for one day.

Rather than check on my neighbor, I hauled Anya out of the car, gave her a snack, changed her diaper, and put her in her crib for a nap. Once that was done, I went downstairs and lifted our new mums out of the car. Rather than put them into the garage, I positioned all of them on the lawn in the locations where I hoped to have them planted. Maybe we could even do it tomorrow. In my mind, I conjured up a fun family activity that would bestow lovely memories on us for years to come. George would dig the holes, I'd plant the flowers, and Anya would see her parents working together as a team.

By the time the mums were in place, I was covered in dirt. A long hot shower was in order. Scrubbed clean, I pulled on an old pair of maternity pants and one of George's out-grown, long-sleeved Henley shirts that he'd put aside for Goodwill. There was a bit of a nip in the air, perfect weather for starting a fire in our new fireplace.

George had purchased a load of wood from a scruffy man, who'd pulled up in a battered truck. Most of the pile sat outside on the pavement at the back of the driveway, but he'd thoughtfully put a half dozen logs in the garage, so they'd be dry and ready to use. I chose three nice ones. Now, I needed a way to encourage them to catch fire.

I dug around in our trash, pulled out a handful of dryer lint, stuffed that into an empty toilet paper roll, and put that under three logs to get them started. After the bark caught, I closed the glass doors and admired the baby fire. All my years as a Girl

Scout had paid off. My fire-making skills were admirable, and the lint and TP roll trick was working perfectly.

Back in the kitchen, I pulled out a small saucepan to heat a cup of apple cider. After adding a cinnamon candy, I stirred the golden liquid gently.

I figured I had a good hour or so to myself, but the baby monitor alerted me to the fact that Anya was awake. I could have left her, hoping that she'd fall back asleep, but I also heard a strange crinkling sound. Better safe than sorry. After turning the burner to low, I ran up the stairs to retrieve my daughter.

In the middle of her crib sat Anya, bare-bottomed and proud, waving a soaked diaper over her head. She'd also managed to soak her sheets.

"Okay, young lady, let's rinse you off," I said as I whisked her into the bathroom for a quick bath.

She was totally undressed when the smoke alarm went off.

29

*T*he gizmo shrieked at a decibel that sent me staggering around the bathroom. Anya was buck naked, so I grabbed the towel and swaddled her. All my hurrying and the loud noise upset her, and she began to cry.

To add to the din, the doorbell rang.

I clutched my child to my chest and trooped down the stairs. Without looking through the keyhole, I opened the front door to find a man on my front step. He was short and stocky, under a mop of bright red hair.

"I'm Detective Everbright from the Ladue Police Department. Do you always open your door without checking to see who's out here? That's not a good idea."

I could barely hear him over the shriek of the smoke alarm. As he spoke, he pulled a wallet from his coat pocket and flipped it open. I glanced long enough to see he was who he said he was.

Anya clamped both hands over her ears and buried her face in my shoulder.

"Pardon?" I thought I heard what he was saying, but I couldn't be sure.

"Sounds like your smoke alarms are going off. Do you need help?"

The smell of smoke had gotten intense. A coughing fit made it hard for me to spit out the words, "My fireplace..."

Detective Everbright pushed past me and ran inside. I followed him far enough to see a cloud of smoke billowing out of the fireplace. I intended to offer my help, but Anya's cough changed my mind. My eyes watered so badly that it was hard to see. I stumbled my way back to our foyer.

With my body, I propped open the front door. Fortunately, the smoke was not getting thicker. Then came the scrape and clang of metal on metal. The cop reappeared and took me by the elbow.

"Let's get you out in the fresh air. The vent was closed. I assume it's new? You'd never used it? I found a pot on your stove. The contents had boiled over. I opened up your back door, turned on the fan in your kitchen. This place should be aired out in no time."

"Thank you." Hugging Anya closer to me, I shivered.

The cop gently wrapped his jacket around my shoulders. "Let's go sit in my car. Give it ten minutes, and the place should be habitable again."

I followed him to the unmarked police cruiser. "Are you going to give me a ticket?"

"For what?"

"The fireplace? And the stove?"

"No, ma'am. I'm not even going to lecture you. Seems to me you have your hands full. I remember what it was like, when my two girls were small. All hands on deck, 24/7. Is your daughter all right?"

I suddenly remembered that Anya was wearing a towel. "I think so. She had wet herself. That's how I got distracted. I was going to give her a quick bath. Of course, I didn't realize the vent on the fireplace was closed. Stupid me."

"Could have happened to anyone. Especially since it looks like you were using it for the first time. Just glad I came by, when I did."

"I'm lucky you heard the fire alarm and stopped."

He rubbed his chin thoughtfully. "That's not what happened. I'm following up on your neighbor, Sven Nordstrom. You're the person who called 911. Is that right?"

"Yes. I hope he's okay. My husband says he's an ace biker, but that's the second time I've seen him take a tumble. One other time, he nearly ran into Anya while she was in her stroller."

Anya made a grab for the cop's pen and tried to wrestle it out of his hand.

"It's okay. Let her play with it." He clicked the ballpoint into hiding and gave the pen to her. "I think your house should be fine now. Would it be all right, if I ask you a few more questions?"

30

*A*nya and I waited in the car, while Everbright checked the status of the house. He came back carrying the afghan from our sofa for me to use as a cloak. After I handed him back his jacket, he wrapped Anya and me in the crocheted throw. I found his kindness oddly touching. Instead of laughing at my predicament or chiding me, he'd been nothing but nice.

I'd always heard you shouldn't talk to cops, not without an attorney. Everyone says it's just too easy to have your words twisted. But Everbright had rescued me and my baby. Surely I owed him the courtesy of answering a few measly questions.

Once we were all three back inside and a nice fire roared in the fireplace, I asked if he'd mind waiting for me to rinse Anya off and put her back down for the rest of her nap. I had a hunch that, after her long and eventful day, she'd sleep straight through to dinner.

While I finished getting her settled, Everbright had made himself comfortable at my kitchen table and even poured himself a cup of coffee. "Hope you don't mind. Let's go back to the beginning and tell me everything. That might seem tedious or silly to you, but I hope you'll bear with me. Sometimes I'll seize upon a bit of information that seems insignificant to you but meaningful to me, especially when I put all the pieces together. So, if you'll indulge me, I'd like you to tell me everything. From the moment you first became aware of the Nordstroms to this very minute, right now. Can you do that, Mrs. Lowenstein? And by the way, is your Christian name Kiki? Or is that a nickname for Catherine?"

"It's just plain Kiki. That's it; that's all."

Outside the dying leaves rustled on the maple tree. The wonderful fragrance of freshly ground Kaldi's coffee beans scented the air, but there was also the scent of burned apples and wood. I plated the last of the Kaldi's iced cookies and pushed them closer to the cop. "Sure. Why not. But it's kind of a long story."

"Take your time."

Turning on the oven, I set it to bake.

"Do you mind if I work while we talk? I sort of have a mess going here."

"No problem." Everbright had that shabby, unkempt Columbo look about him, as though he'd cultivated such a disheveled image on purpose. His leather belt held up his pants, and the hems hovered above his shoes, allowing an inch of his socks to show. One jacket button dangled precariously from a fuzzy thread. His cuffs were worn and threadbare.

But he must be very, very good at his job, or the powers-that-be in Ladue wouldn't have put up with him. In fact, he didn't match my expectation of a Ladue cop at all. Ladue is the priciest suburb in the metro-St. Louis area. Lots here typically start at a half-a-million dollars and go up. Ladue likes its image as the best of the best, and no one meeting Everbright would think him to be top-notch. At least, not if appearances were all that counted.

After I filled a second cup of coffee for him, the detective sipped his drink, had a couple of cookies, and took copious notes. I put a tray of slice-and-bake chocolate cookies in the oven and unpacked boxes marked MISC. while I talked for what seemed like forever, explaining how we'd moved into the house before it was really done, how the Nordstroms complained about the mess our workers made, how Sven nearly ran over Anya in her stroller, and, finally, how I'd really truly made an effort to charm them, but Leesa had been horrible. Just awful.

Each time I thought we were done, he'd ask another question. At last I said, "That brings us to the present. Would you like another cup of coffee? The chocolate chip cookies are almost cool."

"No, thank you," Detective Everbright said. He'd eaten three of the iced cookies I'd gotten from Kaldi's, but I decided not to hold that against him. When he stood up, his eyes bored a hole in me, the way a collector pins a bug to a corkboard. "If there's anything else you remember, I would appreciate a prompt phone call."

"Isn't this a lot for a simple tumble off a bike? I've fallen off my bike before, and no one seemed to care. Of course, I didn't need an ambulance, but..." I paused as I realized why Everbright was so very, very interested in Sven's accident. "Does this mean you think Sven Nordstrom's accident wasn't really an accident after all? Was he drugged or something, when he fell off his bike?"

31

There was a shrewd closing up of the detective's face. His changing expression suggested he was totally aware that he didn't look overly bright — and that he used this misdirection to his advantage. Carefully, he weighed his words.

"It means that Mr. Nordstrom's accident is under investigation. I'm talking to you now, Mrs. Lowenstein, because all the details are fresh in your mind. You're the person who found him lying there on the ground. You called the ambulance. You're the best eyewitness I have."

"But that word — eyewitness — it implies a person who saw something important. Something worth reporting in detail. Are you telling me that Sven Nordstrom has been seriously hurt?"

"No."

"Is he sick? Is it contagious? Should I take Anya to the doctor?"

"No, Mr. Nordstrom is not contagious, at least not to my knowledge."

Everbright reached into his back pocket and pulled out a business card. "Call me if you happen to remember —"

I bit back a sense of irritation. I'd spent nearly an hour with this cop, going over every detail of our lives since we'd moved into this house, and he was giving me the brush-off. That didn't seem fair. "Rather than waste time with me, why don't you just ask Sven what happened?"

"I wish I could," Everbright said in a wistful way, "but he's unable to talk. He's pretty out of it. You've been very kind, Mrs. Lowenstein. I am sorry that I've taken so much of your day. Especially seeing as how you've got so much work to do."

"Whoa! This card says homicide investigator! You didn't tell me that! Is Sven dead?"

Everbright shook his head slowly. "No, and with any luck he'll be just fine. See, when a person has a suspicious accident, we often ask a lot of questions at the start. That way, if things go south, we have the sort of information we need to proceed successfully."

I clamped a hand over my mouth. "Things go south? You're trying to tell me that Sven won't make it."

"I didn't say that, and please don't jump to conclusions. We are simply being cautious. That's all."

After Everbright left, I continued to put away linens and pots. I knew I should tackle the big box labeled DINNERWARE, but I couldn't face the task. Suddenly, I felt totally depleted.

I knew why. Everbright had come and gone, and he'd left me with the worrisome possibility that Sven's fall off his bike had been something much more sinister than a loss of balance. Okay, I felt sorry for Sven, and maybe a little sorry for Leesa, too, but, mostly, I was scared. Not for me, but for Anya.

And it occurred to me, once again, how alone I was. I tried to call George and got his voicemail. I phoned his office and was told by his secretary, Brandi, that he was out. I thought about calling Sheila but discarded that idea nearly as fast as I considered it.

I had nowhere to turn.

When we had left college, I'd intended to make new friends, once we'd gotten settled, but our first apartment was in a highly transient community. While we waited for this place to be finished, we lived in an extended stay hotel, housing that by its very name explained it was short-term. Thus, we'd moved here with high hopes. Now our closest neighbors had effectively slammed their door in my face.

Or I suppose you could say that the ambulance driver had slammed his door in my face, and Sven had simply been lying there with an IV in his arm.

Details aside, the point remained the same: I badly needed to make new friends.

32

Typically, we spent Friday nights with Sheila, lighting the candles and having our Shabbas ceremony. But shortly after Everbright left, she phoned to say she wasn't feeling well. "I had my flu shot, and I'm running a fever."

"Is there anything I can do for you?" I asked.

"No. I've already phoned George to explain I had to cancel."

I told her I hoped she'd feel better, and we said our goodbyes.

That evening I stayed up as long as possible, hoping to share with George the news of Everbright's visit. Eventually, I fell asleep on the sofa.

My husband must have crept in sometime after three a.m. As a consequence, he decided to sleep late that morning.

I did my best to keep the noise level down. Rather than play Anya's favorite CD full blast on the stereo, I turned it low. Instead of emptying her diaper pail, I waited, since her room was right next to the master bedroom.

Around eleven, I took Anya outside for a quick walk. We ran into Mr. Bergen at the corner. "My, my. It's that pretty little girl and her pretty little girl."

The compliment brought a blush to my face. "That's very sweet of you."

"I'm looking for Bartholomew. He slipped past me this morning, when I stepped out to get my newspaper. That animal is such a rascal. Faster than a car at the Indy 500."

"How old is he?"

"Ten. Bought him for Alma from that pet shop they used to have in the mall. Poor thing sat there by his lonesome, meowing and acting pitiful. Alma begged me to rescue him. I'd never wanted a cat. Don't like 'em. They're sneaky creatures. But I could never say no to Alma. I gave in."

"Where do you think he went?"

"Not far. Probably one of these houses nearby. Bart likes to explore, but he's too old to tomcat around." With that, Mr. Bergen cupped his hands over his mouth and yelled, "Bart? Where are you, you old rascal? Bart?"

"Anya and I will keep our eyes open for you. If you give me your phone number, I'll call you, if we see him."

Mr. Bergen rattled off a local number and I keyed into my phone. After testing it, I told him goodbye and pushed Anya around the block.

We'd completed our circuit and wound up facing the Nordstroms' house when a plane flew overhead.

"Bird!" Anya pointed toward the sky.

Shading my eyes, I looked up. "Plane, honey. That's an airplane."

"Bird," she repeated.

I pushed her past the Nordstroms' garage. Sven's bike had disappeared. However, you could still make out the broken blades of grass where he'd fallen. That shook me to my core. I sent up a prayer for his recovery.

"Bird," Anya insisted defiantly as the roar of the plane overhead grew louder.

"Okay, sweetie, if you say so." I concentrated on getting her over the slight hump where the Nordstroms' driveway met the sidewalk. Because I worried about overturning the stroller, I took every lump and bump slowly.

A flicker of black appeared on the edge of my peripheral vision. I stopped, scanned the Nordstroms' bushes, and looked again at what appeared to be a moving shadow.

But it wasn't.

It was Bart, intent on chasing something in the grass. The black cat was total focused on his prey. He paid no attention as I snuck up behind him. With a swoop, I scooped him up. At the same time, I heard a metallic creak. It startled me and the cat. Bart squirmed in my arms, jumped to the ground, and took off running.

To my surprise, the Nordstroms' garage door creaked open.

I stayed put, expecting to see a car pull up. Bart disappeared in the overgrown weeds at the edge of our lot.

Even though I waited, no vehicle approached. No cars were on the street. No person stood nearby, pointing the opener at the gaping hole.

But the door had definitely gone up.

"Did you see that, Anya?" I took my accustomed place behind her stroller. "The door went up all by itself. Either that, or I'm losing my mind."

33

a s I settled Anya in her high chair for a late lunch, George wandered down the stairs. His hair was wet. He smelled like he'd freshly showered. He puttered around in the kitchen, brewing himself fresh coffee. He avoided eye contact with me, but he did give Anya a cuddle. After hugging her and depositing her in the highchair, he asked, "Have you unpacked the rest of the coffee mugs, Kiki?"

This was a bit much for a man who had stayed out all night and slept until noon. Admittedly, my feelings were prickly. I'd been burning to share my visit with Detective Everbright. Considering that George didn't do anything around the house, how dare he hassle me about missing coffee cups?

Really, was Everbright's visit any of George's business? My husband had been unavailable, so why should I bother to tell him that the cops were now involved? Huh. He didn't care, did he? If he cared, how could George have gone so long without bothering to check on us?

"Nope. What you see is what there is." I took a jar of Anya's favorite baby food out of the refrigerator, uncapped it, covered it with plastic wrap, and put it in the microwave. On the stovetop, I set a pot of hot water to make macaroni and cheese, but the ugly splotch of the burned apple juice stopped me in my tracks. First I'd need to wipe it down.

Nah.

Instead, I switched burners. The move seemed ironic, because a slow burn was rising from my neck to my face. George was treating me like the hired help. He'd stayed out all night, and his first words were to ask if I'd unboxed coffee mugs? I kept my back to him, fearful that I would yell in frustration, if he even looked at me cross-ways.

A watched pot never boils, but I stood over the saucepan full of water like I'd never heard this axiom, watching anxiously for rising bubbles.

This is your life, Kiki. Your idea of a good time is keeping an eye on a pot of water. You are useful only for menial labor. Your husband doesn't even come home at a decent hour — and, the next morning, he feels no need to explain or apologize. You are a big, fat zero. (Emphasis on the big and fat.)

I hate it when the voice inside my head chews me out. It was symptomatic of being tired, having indulged in wine, and not doing enough for myself. I knew I was teetering on the edge. I knew I needed a break. A little time outside this messy house would be a good start. And I needed an hour or so away from Anya.

But I wasn't about to ask George for help. No way.

That said, I was tired of being ignored by him. Okay, maybe my figure rivaled that of the Pillsbury Dough Boy, but I was young, and Mr. Bergen had said I was pretty. I didn't dress like our slutty neighbor, Leesa. But I also didn't spend much money on my clothes. If I could lose a few pounds, I'd feel better about buying new things. Until then, the shopping trip would have to wait.

I pulled my phone from my pocket and googled local exercise programs. Scrolling past the gyms, I searched for dance-based options. I stopped when I got to Zumba. The colorful green and purple logo struck a chord. In our mailbox, there'd been evidence of a mix-up by the postal delivery person. Sorting through the bills and flyers, I found a large envelope with the Zumba logo, addressed to Leesa, which I'd dutifully returned.

Seeing it now, the bright icon seemed like an invitation to fun. The schedule showed a late afternoon session. Participants could pay a walk-in fee or buy a regular class pass, but you had to arrive fifteen minutes early to complete paperwork. A glance at the clock told me I had two and a half hours to get ready.

"I hope you don't have plans for this afternoon," I said to my husband without bothering to turn around. "I'm going out. Alone."

George had pulled up a chair next to Anya's. I'd heard the legs scraping the floor. Anya was happily banging her spoon on the tray of her high chair. The microwave dinged, signaling the baby food was heated. But the loudest sound was the roar of anger in my head.

"You need me to babysit?" George sounded whiney.

I fought the urge to take the jar of hot baby food and throw it at him. Instead, I clamped my teeth together, hard, and counted to ten. As I emptied the food into a bowl so it could cool, I said, "No. You see, George, when it's your own child, you are not a babysitter. It's called *parenting*. I realize it might interfere with your nighttime ritual of staying out till all hours, but them's the breaks, pal. You have spent exactly zip time with your daughter since we moved. Zip, zilch, nada."

I smiled a nasty smile. "Now you have a choice to make. Either you spend time with her, or you continue to turn your back on her. If you decide on the latter, don't expect Anya to run to you when she needs someone. She'll come to me. That's okay, because I'll always be here for her, but you're going to miss out on what it means to be a father. And, buddy, you're coming awfully close to letting that particular barn door slam shut behind you. Keep it up, and you'll have bailed out on the most important relationship of your life."

He literally gasped. The blood drained from his face. Hearing the boiling water rattle the pot, I poured in the pasta.

Anya quit banging her spoon. Her lively eyes moved from me to George and back to me. Okay, she couldn't parse the words, but she knew something significant had happened.

"I, uh..." He stopped. "Work and then..."

I stared him down. "Frankly, I don't care where you were or what you did. Nor am I interested in hearing you lie about it. But I do care about our daughter."

With that, I set the bowl of baby food down in front of Anya.

"You probably don't realize this, but Anya loves Kraft Macaroni and Cheese. You can finish it up for her. The macaroni is in the pot. Just follow the directions on the box," I said, and I walked out of the room.

34

*a*fter making an exit like that, you can't turn around and walk back into the room. It's anti-climactic. Besides, George needed to stew in his own juices. If I did an about-face and re-entered the kitchen, he'd be off the hook, and that would negate everything I'd said.

My only option was to grab my keys and go for a drive. As I hoisted my purse over one shoulder, I also grabbed the diaper bag, before realizing that I wouldn't need it. Suddenly, I recognized, with terrible clarity, that I'd grown accustomed to having Anya by my side. So much so that going anywhere without her felt wrong, as if the hook-side of the Velcro surrounding my heart had been ripped free from its corresponding loops. The freedom versus the isolation hit me with a one-two emotional punch. I'd grown too dependent on my baby. While I had always thought that she needed me, I'd come to rely on her, too. Anya had become my "lovey," fulfilling for me what her stuffed rabbit did for her.

The pull to see her was seismic. I had to force myself to walk down the hall that ran along to the side door. On my way to the car, I stopped in the laundry room and dug around in a box labeled EXERCISE CLOTHES. Those words had been written with a thick Sharpie, because I'd been overly optimistic. In my dreams, our move would magically change me from a slightly overweight housewife to an organized and efficient, slim and trim, young mother who belonged here in tony Ladue. The box had become emblematic of those dreams, as I'd gone online and purchased a pair of exercise pants and cute top to match my fantasies. All I needed to become that totally fit woman was a pair of shoes and socks.

Tucking the togs under one arm, I exited our side door and climbed into my car. Once there, my automatic impulse was to turn and check on Anya, making sure she was securely fastened in her car seat.

But, of course, Anya was inside the house with her father.

The recognition that I relied on her so entirely shook me to my very core.

This was not right. Instinctively, I realized that if I didn't build a life for myself outside the orb of my child's world, I would cripple both of us. She would sense this neediness of mine. It would keep her from venturing forth, as surely as a chain keeps a dog tethered to a doghouse in a backyard. And for me, the attachment would prove equally disastrous. I would long for her, depend on her, and need her, rather than provide a launching pad for her.

Humbled by this, I keyed the ignition and backed out slowly. I had no idea where I would go except to buy those shoes and socks and show up for the Zumba class. No friend to visit. Nowhere to stop and say, "Hi!" That also shook me to the core. I knew I needed a life outside my house, but where was I going to find one?

After inching the car to the end of the driveway, I panicked. I needed to let George assume his role as Anya's father and to give

Anya a relationship with her dad. But what could I do for myself? *Where, oh where, would I find Kiki?*

There was nothing to do but venture forth, in search of the person I might become.

At the corner, I spotted Mr. Bergen. One hand rested on a cane, and the other was jammed deep in his pants pocket. I rolled down a window. "Hi, Mr. Bergen. How are you and Bart?"

"That rascal. He's gone and run off again."

This seemed to be the ongoing dance of their lives, a complex pattern they followed day after day.

"I'll be extra careful driving and keep an eye out for your kitty."

He nodded. "You do that, girlie."

35

a stop at DSW proved fruitful. I found a pair of shoes intended for aerobic dancing. The sole was flat enough to accommodate turning and spinning. The salesgirl pointed out socks on sale, and I snapped up a couple of pairs. Next I ran into the nearest CVS. I bought a cheap refillable water bottle, an energy bar, an inexpensive purse-sized hairbrush, and a new scrunchie. Thus armed, I slicked my hair back off my face, gobbled down the energy bar — which must be a new name for candy bar — and headed for the gym's parking lot.

How was I going to fill the hour before the class started?

A Michaels Crafts store and a Barnes & Noble Booksellers occupied the same plaza as the gym. With a cautious enthusiasm, I headed for those two stores.

Inside Michaels, I wandered around and admired all the Halloween décor items. A few were too spooky for Anya, but a couple might tickle her fancy. I chose a talking owl and a silly witch that you could hang in your window.

The scrapbooking aisle intrigued me, especially when I noticed a book called *Scrapbook Storytelling* by Joanna Campbell Slan. It explained simple ways to save all sorts of memories. I put it in the cart, found a cheap notebook on sale, and decided I would do better at taking pictures of Anya and writing down her adventures. Somewhere in my belongings, I had a book that my nana had made for me by sewing together pieces of black cotton fabric and gluing on pictures from magazines. Michaels didn't have much in the way of fabric, but I picked up a tube of E-6000 glue. Until if could visit a fabric store, at least I could start saving pictures.

Inside Barnes & Noble, I realized they had more stationery, toys, and gifts than books. That made me sad. However, I found the mystery aisle and picked up a few new paperbacks.

Having wasted a little time so pleasantly, I gathered my purchases and walked to the car. Alternately, I felt liberated and guilty. I hadn't earned any of the money I'd spent. It was George's. Or was it? Hadn't we agreed that I'd stay home with our child? Wasn't it up to me to feed her, bathe her, entertain her, schedule her doctor visits, and get up with her at night?

Did that count as a job?

I wasn't exactly sure.

36

"Fill this out." An incredibly muscular young woman pushed a clipboard with a form my way. A pen dangled from a string tied to the clip.

The girl didn't seem particularly interested in me. After shoving the paperwork my way, she went back to texting on her phone. Her thumbs, with their chipped orange polish, were moving at a lightning fast speed.

After signing my name to a promise that I was in generally good health and that I didn't intend to drop dead in the middle of a class and that if I did I wouldn't sue them — although how I could sue them if I were dead eluded me — I handed the clipboard back to the girl, who'd since pinned on a nametag that said, "Sandy."

"That'll be twenty bucks. Cash." Her open palm waited for the money.

"I thought my first session was free. That's what it says on your website."

She narrowed her eyes. Her smile disappeared. "Oh. I forgot."

Somehow that rang hollow. I had a mental image of Sandy

pocketing the odd twenty dollar bill several times a week. She had a nice scam going.

Rather than ask where the changing room was or where the class would be held, I walked past Sandy, as though I was already a member. The locker room seemed clean enough. I found an empty spot in the back and changed my clothes. The stretchy exercise clothes emphasized all my lumps and bumps. In the mirror, a black and purple sausage stared back at me.

"I'm in the right place," I told the pathetic-looking woman in the mirror. "Because if I start exercising regularly, those lumps and bumps are sure to disappear."

After that, I avoided my reflection. That woman in the mirror had her life, and I had mine. I put on my new socks and shoes. Shoving my purse into a locker, I twisted the key attached to a plastic bracelet and tested the door to see that I had, indeed, locked the metal vault. I filled my new bottle with cold tap water and took a deep breath.

Time to hit the dance floor!

37

One other woman was waiting in the classroom. She'd spread a yoga mat on the floor and begun by assuming a kneeling pose. I skirted around her, found a spot nearby and sat down. When she un-pretzeled herself, she noticed me. "Hi, I'm Maggie Earhart. You're new, right?"

"Yes." I introduced myself.

"You didn't hand over twenty bucks to Sandy, did you?"

"Nope."

"That girl. The only reason they don't fire her is that she's the owner's niece. What a sneaky little thief. I bet she didn't warn you about the teacher either."

Uh-oh. A tingle swept over my body. "Warn me about the teacher. Um, no. She didn't. What is it I should know?"

Maggie waved a hand in the air. She had adorable freckles sprinkled over her nose. Her green-blue eyes danced with merriment. Like me, she'd slicked back all her hair, capturing it with a coated rubber band. "Let's say she has mood swings."

I blinked. I couldn't think of anything appropriate to say. Fortunately, I didn't have to. Maggie kept on talking. "Her name is Leesa Nordstrom, and she's from Norway or Denmark or some other frozen land of Vikings. She thinks she's perfection itself. I'll admit she's got a body that doesn't stop, but she's not much of a teacher. Oh, she gets up there and dances, but she doesn't give you any direction at all. Doesn't call the steps before they happen. Since you're new, you might want to stand up front, so you can follow her. Otherwise, until you know the songs, you'll probably be lost."

I sincerely doubted that Leesa would be joining us, seeing that her husband was in hospital, but rather than share my inside knowledge, I decided to stay mum. "That's great advice. But I wouldn't be comfortable up front. Not with everybody staring at me. Even if I miss a step or two, I'd rather be in the back. Where does Leesa stand?"

Maggie pointed to the far end of the room. She also told me where I could find a mat, because I'd need one for the last ten minutes of the class, the cool down.

"Have you ever taken a Zumba class before?"

"I've watched them on TV," I said. "But never taken one live. This'll be a new experience for me."

"I love the Latin music. It's so energizing. I started with another girl, Grenata. She was terrific. Very friendly, got to know your name, broke down the hard steps for you, eager to praise anyone for anything. Yes, Grenata was wonderful. You left feeling so upbeat we called her the 'human high.'"

"When does she teach?"

A woman walked in and took a spot a few feet to the right of me.

Maggie gave the newcomer a tiny wave of greeting. Turning sad eyes to me, my new friend shook her head. "Grenata doesn't teach anymore. She's dead."

38

That set my heart racing, even before Leesa bounced into the room. She wore skin-tight pants and a top that looked like a slasher had attacked it with scissors. Underneath the open-air tee was a snug bra top. Like most of us, she'd pulled back her hair. Unlike most of us, she'd applied her makeup with a trowel.

A trio of similarly dressed young women walked in with Leesa. They took all the prime spots in the front of the class. The first five minutes of our one-hour session were spent with Leesa fiddling with the sound system. Her back stayed to us, and she didn't appear to be in any hurry. Nor did she offer any apologies.

I glanced over at Maggie, who shrugged at me in a "what-are-you-going-to-do?" sort of way.

We waited patiently. At one point, Leesa stood up and did a head count. When she got to me, her mouth fell open. "You? You are here?" Her tone was faintly accusatory.

That ticked me off. I'd rushed to her husband's aid. I'd called the ambulance for him. I knew he was in the hospital and I wondered why on earth his wife felt it incumbent on her to go ahead and teach a silly exercise class under the circumstances.

"Yes," I said firmly. "I am here."

With a sneer, she went back to the sound system.

"What was *that* all about?" asked Maggie.

But I never had the chance to answer, because Leesa finally got the right tunes cued up. Once she heard the opening strains, she cranked the volume as loud as it would go. The mirrors on the surrounding walls shivered to the deep vibrations of the bass. With her back to us, as though none of us existed, Leesa began a series of warm-up moves that could best be called provocative. More accurately, I found them embarrassing. The fingers trailing over our private parts, the sensual tossing of our heads, well, it was a bit much — and our instructor seemed to retreat into her own tiny world. We ceased to exist.

The music changed abruptly. A gleeful Latin tune surrounded us. "New song," announced Leesa. Now she moved like the instructors I'd seen on TV. She plunged into a series of steps that I found easy enough to follow. The steps Leesa was doing were nothing particularly difficult, but if you'd never seen them before, they would be confusing. Most of the students lost their way. Leesa's special friends kept up with her. So did I.

The third song must have been an old favorite, because nearly everyone followed along happily.

Then came another complex number with a sequence that totally baffled Leesa's posse. I missed the steps the first time through, but the second round, I knew instinctively when to step and when to pause. Next came a set of moves that culminated with a change of direction. Suddenly, I stood at the front of the class instead of the back. In the mirror's reflection, I watched Leesa's eyes focus on me. She followed my moves carefully. Clearly, she expected me to fail in my new position at the head of the class.

But I didn't. Smoothly, flawlessly, I led us through the chore-ography. In fact, I even put my own flare in the steps, a nice touch, because Leesa moved in a sort of herky-jerky way that looked clumsy. She lacked what dancers call "quality of movement." Obviously, she'd come to dancing late in life. She didn't understand that energy flows from inside your core to the outside of your body.

For example, Leesa would stick her hand in the air, while mine would float there. She would put her foot on the floor, while mine would slide there. Her body seemed stubby while mine looked elongated.

Once she realized I was innately better than she, Leesa watched me like a burning intensity. An extra propulsion of anger fueled her steps, turning them more awkward than they needed to be.

Since I hadn't danced in practically forever, when we reached the fifteen minute mark, I huffed and puffed. But I didn't care. Despite the toll the exertion was taking on my wind, I kept up with Leesa. I gave myself over to the music, flowing with it. By contrast, she grew more and more perturbed, and it made her clumsy.

At the end of the hour, I was exhausted. Nevertheless, I felt deeply satisfied. I was keeping up. The others were falling behind. Leesa had taken to barking orders. A snarl marred her pretty face. I, on the other hand, felt joyful. A glance in the mirror confirmed I was drenched and glowing.

I really did need to do this more often!

39

"*W*ay to go!" Maggie gave me a big grin and a slap on the back. "I usually head over to Panera Bread after class. Want to join me?"

"I would love to, but I have a little one at home."

"You sure? We worked off a ton of calories."

Before I could answer, Leesa bowled into Maggie, practically shoving her out of the way. "You," she said as drops of spittle landed on my face, "you are stalker. You follow me. You spy on me."

"Lucky thing, huh? I was there when your husband fell off his bike. If it hadn't been for me, no one would have called for help. He might still be lying there in the grass."

"I say he fall because of you! We had nice neighborhood until you come."

"Really?" I shook my head. "Leesa, I've had enough of you. Grow up!"

"Grow up? Like you? Fat woman? I see you in my class, and I laugh. You look funny, like kielbasa that tries to dance."

"Whoa," Maggie stepped forward, "Leesa, you are seriously

crossing a line here. You have no right to speak to her like that. None. I'll report you to management."

"Say what you want. I am best teacher ever. They know that. They will not listen to you. Where will they find another teacher good like me? They will not ever."

"Is that so? Honest to Pete." Maggie shook her head.

"Who is Pete?" Leesa glanced around. "Where is this Pete? I talk to him."

It was too much. I laughed so hard that I couldn't stop. Rather than fall down, I grabbed Maggie. She held onto me, and our laughter proved infectious. The two of us staggered out of the classroom, while Leesa screamed what I assume were obscenities in her native tongue.

"Bread Co. here we come," I said as I unlocked the door of my BMW. "After that, dinner's on me, Maggie."

"I'll lead the way." She hopped in her car.

40

*A*lthough the proper name is St. Louis Bread Company, everyone in the area calls it "Bread Co." to rhyme with "Bread Dough." The chain is one of my personal favorite places, and it has many locations scattered around the city and suburbs. Maggie showed me a back route that brought us to a Bread Co. not far from CALA, the Charles and Anne Lindbergh Academy, a fancy private school.

"I teach at CALA," Maggie explained once we were inside. "Right now, I'm only a substitute. I hope to get on full time. The position comes with a discounted tuition for teachers' kids. CALA is terrific, but it's also very pricey."

"My husband and his mother are both alums," I said.

"Sheila Lowenstein is your mother-in-law? Wow. Should we leave and go someplace where you can get a stiff drink?"

"Sugar will do the job for me," I said with a giggle.

We joined the line of patrons placing their orders. Maggie had a "You Pick Two" combo of broccoli cheese soup and a turkey sandwich. It sounded so warm and filling that I ordered the same. We settled on iced green tea for our drinks. I gladly paid. Once we found a booth in the back, we settled in to wait for our names to be called so we could pick up our orders.

"How long have you been taking Zumba?" I asked.

"Two years now. Like I told you earlier, my first teacher was Grenata. Gosh, she and Leesa were different as night and day. Grenata made the class so much fun. Best of all, she really liked her students. Grenata knew our names. On our birthdays, she'd let us pick our favorite songs, and she'd play them as a special treat."

I was impressed and said as much.

"Yeah, it was a real bummer when she lost her job."

"You said that she died."

"Right, but before she was diagnosed, Leesa took her place. We all think that Leesa got Grenata in trouble. I've heard rumors that Leesa told management that Grenata wasn't officially registered with Zumba as an instructor. That was a lie, but the manager didn't bother to check. He gave Grenata the boot. I mean, he showed her the bottom of his tennis shoe. Didn't even give her a chance to stand up for herself." Maggie stirred the ice in her green tea. "That was bad enough. Then we heard that Grenata had ovarian cancer. After a long fight, she died. It's so sad."

The worker behind the counter called our names. Maggie and I got up to grab our trays. She caught me sneaking a peek at my cell phone.

"Worried about your sitter?"

"The sitter is my husband. He's never taken care of our daughter this long before."

"Take it from me, mother of two. Stay out as long as you can."

I must have looked astonished.

"I'm not kidding, Kiki. If you hurry back, he can avoid doing all sorts of yucky stuff, like changing a dirty diaper. But if you stay out, he'll be forced to roll up his sleeves and dig in. That's good. For him and your baby. It's too easy for the dads to pawn our children off on us, especially if we're stay-at-home-moms. When they do, they miss out on all those special moments, like when your little one smiles at you after a diaper change. Or how adorable your kid looks after a nice bath. It might feel like you're cheating by leaving them together, but the truth is that you're cheating *them,* if you don't give them the chance to bond."

Her words rang with the conviction of hard-won truth. As we walked back to our booth, she walked back her commentary. "Look, I didn't mean to lecture you. Tell me, how do you know Leesa? I got the impression you two had met before."

"First, you don't need to apologize. I can see where you're coming from, and I think you are right. George and Anya need to spend more time together. Second, Leesa is my neighbor." With that introduction, I told Maggie about all the problems we'd had since moving in. I finished with, "I can't believe she came to class, even though her husband is in the hospital. I'd be worried sick. Of course, maybe that's exactly why she *did* come. The class would have been a good distraction."

"Right." Maggie tapped a fingernail on the table top. "Like she needs a distraction. Truth is, Leesa cares about one person and one person only, and that person's name is Leesa. I've never seen such a self-absorbed person in my life. Did you notice that she rarely ever glanced at us? No, ma'am. She was totally focused on one person in that class – Leesa. If that song hadn't forced us to turn around, she would never have noticed you are a terrific dancer."

I shrugged. "I took a lot of dance when I was young. I love it. What a workout!"

"Since you've taken lessons before, you had to have noticed Leesa is not much of a teacher. She's collecting money and showing up for her own benefit. The rest of us are just along for the ride."

"Maybe she teaches as a way to keep up with her husband. Her husband is this fantastic bicycle rider. He goes miles and miles every day. That guy doesn't have one ounce of fat on his body."

"If she cared about him that would make sense." Maggie sucked in a deep sigh and let it out slowly. "But she doesn't. She's a shameless flirt. Her husband has come into the gym many, many times. He's seen her rubbing up against the other men, flirting with them, and being a tease. They've even had words about it. Public fights. They don't seem to care who hears them."

I stored all this away.

Tomorrow I would phone Detective Everbright.

41

*M*aggie and I exchanged phone numbers and promised to get back in touch, although we agreed that might be difficult. She lived in the far western suburbs, and I lived near the heart of the city. Once we figured out that our kids were close in age, we agreed that the long drive was unimportant. When I told her goodbye, I felt good. I'd finally made a new friend. Sort of. At least I was on my way.

I got home at eight. I expected recriminations from George, but when I walked to the great room I found him huddled with Anya on the sofa. He was reading *Goodnight Moon* to her.

If I live to be one hundred, I will never forget that image of the two of them, their heads bowed over the pages, her little fingers curled over his big hand as he propped the book up so they both could see it. It is, in fact, the dearest moment of my life to date. Whatever else George was or wasn't, he was certainly an adoring dad. He treated his child as if she were made of delicate blown glass. At this special moment, he gave her his full and total attention.

In the illumination of a lamp he'd perched on top of a box, George's face was a study in light and shadows. I stared at his strong nose and chin, the lock of hair that wouldn't lie down on his crown, and his dazzling blue eyes framed with long lashes. Anya had his coloring, his intensity, but her features had softened when mixed up with mine, so that her nose was smaller and more delicate. Her chin was firm but not chiseled. I knew, without seeing them, that her eyes were as blue as his.

Since they didn't notice me right away, I lingered in the shadows. A box hid me from their view.

"Where is that mouse?" George asked. "I think he's on every page. Do you see him, Anya?"

"Da." She stabbed the page with a tiny index finger.

"Smart girl. That's right. The mouse is hiding, isn't he? Do you see a clock in the room? You probably don't know what a clock is, do you, sweetheart? You've never seen one. We'll have to buy one, won't we? Just so you'll understand. This is a clock. See? You use it to tell time. Like when it's time to go to bed."

"Be-ah?"

"Bed."

I stepped into the light. "Bedtime is right about now, Anya-Banana."

George smiled up at me. "I fed Anya dinner and wiped her face, but I didn't feel confident enough to give her a bath by myself. Will you show me how? I'm scared to death I'll get water in her nose."

"Of course." I held out my arms and Anya climbed up to snuggle against me. She wasn't exactly dressed for bed. He'd changed her into a play outfit that could have fooled anyone except a mother. The big buttons on the front would not have been comfortable for snoozing. "Does she need a clean diaper?"

"I changed her ten minutes ago. Actually, I've changed her several times. The first time, I guess I had her diaper on backwards, because I got a soaking. The second, I ruined the tape.

You might want to check up on me. I'd hate to have her diaper fall off in the middle of the night."

"Will do." I turned away, heading for the stairs.

"Kiki?" he called after me. "Wait a minute. Let me give her a goodnight kiss first, okay?"

He joined us. To my surprise, he wrapped his arms around both Anya and me. "My girls," he said in a husky voice. "The women in my life. I love you both."

I was so stunned, I thought I'd fall over.

42

*a*fter we put Anya to bed, George asked, "How was your afternoon? Have you had any dinner? I didn't get the chance to eat. If you'd like, I'll make you something, too."

That was incredibly thoughtful of him, and I said so. In the kitchen, I handed over the bag of pastries from Bread Co. We sat across from each other at the kitchen table, while he ate a Reuben sandwich.

Before I could tell him my news about Detective Everbright's visit, he said, "I got an update on Sven Nordstrom. His sister's here from Minnesota. I think her name is Brita. Anya and I saw her while we were out for a walk. Sven's not doing well. In fact, they don't think he's going to make it. He suffered a brain injury called a *coup contrecoup*. Basically, your brain sloshes around inside your skull. When you smack down hard, it jostles one way and rebounds the other. That causes an injury to both sides."

George picked up his dish and loaded it into the dishwasher.

"I heard a similar report," and I told George about the visit from Everbright.

George shook his head; those blue eyes of his turned the

color of frozen ice. He sank down into the chair across from mine. "Kiki, you shouldn't have been so honest with him. We know nothing about Everbright. What if he was pumping you to get information? What if you inadvertently said something he took wrong?"

My exercise session and time with Maggie had made me bold. George had a lot of nerve criticizing me, especially in such a scolding tone.

"Okay, George. Here's what you're failing to consider: I never, ever have any adult companionship. No one to talk to. When I do talk, usually no one listens. Yeah, I probably was far too trusting. I don't see any way that Everbright could misinterpret anything that happened. So Sven fell off his bike, and I called for help. Big deal. Isn't that proof of my good intentions? I wasn't even on Sven's side of the street when he fell. Did I mess up? Maybe. But in the big scheme of things, should I blame myself? Nope. It's not my fault you're never available, your mother treats me like dirt, and I spend most of my waking hours all by myself."

The hard look he'd been giving me vanished.

I thought about telling him what I'd learned about Leesa, but I had run out of energy. The high I'd felt after the exercise class was wearing off. A wave of exhaustion hit me.

For what seemed like an eternity, neither George nor I spoke. Finally, he said, "I can see why you're upset with me. In fact, I've been meaning to tell you I know I need to make more of an effort. Taking care of Anya tonight, it hit home that staying here with her isn't a vacation. She's a lot of work. Twice I turned my back and discovered she'd gotten into mischief. I was pretty proud of myself for unpacking that bouncy walker of hers. She went scooting around the floor. Had a grand time, until she found a piece of unprinted newsprint paper and tried to eat it. I had to fish around inside her mouth to get her to give it up. While I was picking up more of the same, she discovered an extension cord. I'd strung it over the counter and onto the kitchen table to charge my laptop. I turned around to see her gumming it. Scared me to death."

"Can you believe what a little monkey she is? Smart and fast and curious. Because her new teeth are coming in, she's eager to test them on whatever comes her way."

I told him about meeting Mert at Home Depot. When I got to the part about the vacuum cleaner sucking up the candy, I thought George was going to pass out.

"The good news is I think I've found a cleaning lady. She'll work us into the next opening on her schedule. I've also learned exactly how to get a stray object out of a child's nose. After we came home, I googled it. The modified vacuum cleaner hose process comes highly recommended. If I'd taken her to the ER, they might have dug around for it."

"Don't even tell me." George covered his face in his hands. "That is completely gross."

"And needlessly expensive. And painful."

"Let's not tell Sheila," he said. Once in a while, he called his mother by her given name. Usually, he did it in conversations like this, when there was a tacit understanding that she was our mutual adversary.

"Agreed."

"Speaking of which, she phoned while you were out. When I told her all that Anya had gotten into, she volunteered to come and get her tomorrow and the next day and so on, until we've made more headway getting organized. I told Mom it was up to you. She said she'd plan on it, unless she heard differently."

"While I hate to impose on her, I think that's the only way I can move ahead. Anya's just too active for me to plop her down in the playpen all day — and I really, really am sick of living in this mess."

"Our mess," George said as he smiled at me. "I don't tell you this enough, but we are partners. You're doing a wonderful job with our baby. She's terrific. So are you."

That night, George and I slept in the same bed. I guess you could say we normalized our relationship. All I know is that I felt happier than I could remember. I didn't fool myself that we were soul-mates, but finding common ground with Anya — and in bed — could be the foundation for a good marriage. Or, at least, that's what I told myself.

43

*a*nya's moving around in her crib woke me up the next morning. I left George sleeping on his stomach, sprawled across our bed. He looked so relaxed that I didn't have the heart to wake him. As I dressed, I stared down at him, remembering the good-looking frat boy who had swept me off my feet at that party three years ago. He had only grown more attractive with age, a process that struck me as incredibly unfair. Men mellowed and grew more debonair. Women wrinkled and closed up like spent flower blossoms dying on the stem.

Tiptoeing into Anya's room, I turned off the baby monitor so my husband could sleep. Since he hadn't bathed her the night before, I gave her a quick rinse in the sink. Once she was clean and sweet-smelling, I dressed her in a cute pair of burnt orange tights and a long brown top, brightened up with leaves in a variety of bright autumnal colors.

A little Velcro bow with an orange ribbon was the perfect accessory. She looked like an ad in a kid's clothing catalog.

We crept down the stairs. For once, she didn't fight me as I slipped her into her high chair.

George joined us in the kitchen. Eager to take advantage of

the good vibes, I said, "If you'll recall, Anya and I went shopping at Home Depot yesterday. You might have noticed the mums out there in the yard."

"Actually, I didn't notice. Did you two have a good time picking out the flowers?" He filled his bowl and carried it to the table. The mood between us was one of harmony. I liked that a lot.

"Yes, we did, didn't we, Anya? She had a great time sniffing them and even tasting one or two. I was thinking that when you get home tonight, we could plant the flowers together. Make it a family ritual. An activity we could share."

"Plant flowers?" He sounded like I'd asked him to dig sewage ditches while chained to a gang of convicts.

"This is the right time of year, and they'll perk up that mud pile with all their bright colors."

"Perk up. Bright colors. Hmmm." George poured milk on his cereal, giving the activity his full attention. He looked up and a slide show of emotions played out on his face. Fatigue. Embarrassment. Guilt. Finally, evasion. Turning to the task of spooning up cornflakes, he said, "I'd love to. Really there's nothing I'd like better, but we're in the middle of this big, big real estate deal. You wouldn't believe the paperwork that goes into a project like this."

I tuned out the rest of the excuse. While he rattled on and on, I grabbed the whisk broom and swept up Cheerios that Anya had scattered on the floor.

George's excuses came to a sputtering end.

"I understand," I said, slamming the broom handle against the wall, as I left it behind and emptied the dustpan into a trash bag.

"Do you? Kiki, I want a sound financial foundation for us. I never want Anya to lack for anything. That's why I work so hard.
"

Right. If that's what you're really doing.

But his plea sounded genuine. I needed to validate my existence, so I told him, "Guess what? I finally got the black marks out of the sink."

There. The sum total of my life's work. I, Kiki Collins Lowenstein, had removed a couple of black marks from our sink. *Woo-hoo.*

"Good." He poured himself another cup of coffee. "That was really bugging me. In fact, I noticed a layer of dust on the dresser in the guest bedroom. The toilets could use cleaning, too. Have you looked out our windows lately? Since they seeded the lawn, there's a layer of dirt on the glass. Also, there are huge dust bunnies under the bed in the guest room."

"Well, then it's a good thing I ran into Mert. Let's keep our fingers crossed she can get here soon."

"Did you check her references?"

"Of course I did."

Of course, I hadn't. But I wasn't about to admit that. I could easily ask Mert for references when I scheduled her visit.

"Sounds like you've got it covered. Okay, I'm off to work." George picked up his briefcase and tossed his jacket over one arm. "Um, and I'll be home late. Big meeting with clients. Don't expect me for dinner."

I choked down the lump in my throat. Rather than make an issue of it, I kept my back to George and tried to sound lighthearted. "Sure. Hope it goes well."

A meeting with clients on a Sunday? I couldn't meet his eyes. How stupid did George think I was?

George was a good provider. Anya was our priority. Maybe I had been unrealistic to hunger for anything more.

44

The knock on the front door came after Anya had gone down for her nap. This time, Everbright didn't ask if he could come in. He simply gave me a curt nod and walked past me.

"Is your husband home?"

The lack of greeting or pre-amble knocked the air out of my lungs. After a ragged breath, I said, "No. You missed him by a couple of hours or so. George has gone into work. He told me he needed to finish up the paperwork on a big deal. He owns Dimont Development downtown in Clayton. But you probably knew that, didn't you?"

Everbright stared at me. "Yes. Yes, I knew that. I was hoping to catch him here."

"Why?"

"To talk."

"About what?"

After George's warning that I shouldn't have spoken so freely to the cop, I was on my guard. Crossing my arms over my chest, I tried to give the impression that I wouldn't be Everbright's patsy again.

"About Mr. Nordstrom."

"What about him?"

I could see that my attitude rubbed Everbright the wrong way. A muscle in his forehead began to pulse. His right fist balled up in a tight knot. We glared at each other for a second, and then he came to a conclusion, one that he didn't share right away. With a long, drawn-out sigh, he gave in. "He's dead."

"What?" My knees buckled beneath me. Everbright grabbed me around the waist and led me through the maze of boxes to my sofa. Once I was seated and propped up with a pillow at my side, he disappeared, only to return with a lukewarm glass of water.

I dutifully took a sip. "Dead? As in, not alive? How did this happen? Must have been a heart attack, right? You hear about cases like that. Seemingly healthy men don't know they have a condition. Even though he was thin, and he cycled all the time, it caught up with him. I bet that first fall was a warning. The second did him in. Or maybe he just had a mild heart attack, and then he did that head-thingie. The *contrecoup*. And that finished him off. It's all because he hit his head. Is that it?"

The cop's smile flickered like a lightbulb before it burns out. That laser beam of intensity was at odds with his slacks, bagged out at the knee, and his shirt, missing one button. "We're not sure what happened. In fact, we don't know the exact cause of death. Not yet. But you are right. Men who seem fine have been known to drop in their tracks of a heart attack. People sometimes die after hitting their heads. It's entirely possible that either scenario is at work here. Or both in concert."

"But that's not what *you* think happened, is it? You believe it was something else, don't you?"

His face turned into an inscrutable mask. "There is nothing I can tell you, Mrs. Lowenstein. On TV, they know all the facts immediately. That's not how it works on real life. Any time a person dies outside of a normal hospital situation, there are questions asked. There will be tests and an autopsy, the whole nine yards. That's procedure, and that's why I'm here today. My job is to gather everything I can, sift through it, and see if a hint of trouble comes to light. If so, we'll investigate further."

I let this sink in. Words stuck out: procedure, questions, autopsy, and investigate. Suddenly I saw the message that had been hidden in plain sight. "Y-y-you think Sven was murdered! You're saying that his death wasn't accidental!"

Everbright's rumpled necktie rose and fell with the weight of his sigh. "I did *not* say that. I don't have enough information to make that determination."

"But that's why you're here, isn't it? You are gathering facts because it's likely Sven Nordstrom was killed —" I stopped. "But that doesn't make any sense. I saw what happened. I was right across the street when he fell off his bike."

"Right." Everbright nodded toward my water glass. "Drink up. The question we need answered is, *Was there a particular reason he fell?* We're looking into the possibility that Mr. Nordstrom was unwell at the time that he came off his bike."

"Unwell," I repeated. "Unwell, as in tampered with? That's what you mean, isn't it? Like purposefully unwell? Like drugged?"

"I don't have an answer to that. If I did, I couldn't share it."

"But you're thinking that someone gave him a shot or a pill, hoping it would make him dizzy enough to fall. If that's the case, what happens next?"

Everbright was standing over me. Taking the empty glass from my hand, he set it on a box and sat next to me. "Do you know if Sven Nordstrom ever had words with your husband?"

"George is hardly ever home. How could he have an argument with the Nordstroms?" I shook my head. "Okay, we were both upset when Sven rode his bicycle too close to Anya's stroller. It scared her and us. But we didn't get into a fight, if that's what you mean by 'had words.' Although we could have. Especially seeing how reckless Sven had been. In fact, despite his stupid behavior, we've gone out of our way to be friendly. I took over a chocolate cake, flowers, and a card. Leesa practically threw them in my face. Even so, George keeps nagging at me to be friendly with *all* our neighbors, especially the Nordstroms."

"Did Mr. Lowenstein mention anything about bumping into Sven Nordstrom one evening? Anything at all?"

Tears turned the world into a messy blur. "I told you about how Sven nearly ran over Anya. That's the only time my husband had contact with Mr. Nordstrom. Ever. At least as far as I know."

"At least as far as you know," Everbright repeated my words back to me. "So you don't know anything about a fight at a restaurant on The Hill? One where they almost came to blows?"

45

"What? George? My George? Fought with Sven? You have to be kidding me. Who told you that?" I wanted to lunge across the sofa, grab Everbright by his wrinkled tie, and shake him until his teeth fell out of his head.

"We have at least a dozen people who saw them."

"When?"

Everbright named a day and date. I opened my phone and checked the calendar function. "That was the day after the Nordstroms had their party."

He consulted his notes. "Yes. I guess your husband and a group of people were having dinner at Antonio's, a restaurant on The Hill, when the Nordstroms walked in. Mr. Lowenstein excused himself and went over to speak to the Nordstroms. People overheard him chastise them for being so rude to you. His exact words were, 'She's been nothing but nice to you, and you've treated her like dirt under your feet.'"

I chewed the air. I couldn't imagine George standing up for me, much less while dining at a classy place in our city's famous Italian district. Sheila had drummed into his head that you never acted impolite in public. George often remarked on people who raised their voices or appeared to be upset in public forums.

But this detective was saying that George had actually violated his own code of behavior to confront the Nordstroms — and on my behalf. The fact that my husband had stood up for me was the most shocking part of Everbright's report. I couldn't imagine George taking my side. Words stuck in my throat, and I had to jump up and run into the kitchen. There, I rustled around in the refrigerator, until I found my stash of Diet Dr Peppers. I pulled one from the plastic holder and popped the top open.

Everbright padded after me into the kitchen. While I chugged the diet cola, he leaned against my doorframe.

"Want one?" I pointed to my can.

"You wouldn't happen to have more coffee? Cookies? I haven't eaten all day."

"Well, for pity's sake," I said, and nearly groaned, because I sounded just like my mother. "Why didn't you say so? We can't have that. How about if I fix you a sandwich? Do you like grilled cheese?"

In reply, his stomach rumbled. "Yes, please."

"Then have a seat, and I'll make you one."

The change of subject lightened the atmosphere considerably. As I put together the bread and cheese, I talked to the cop more casually, while he took a chair at the kitchen table. "George has never, ever stood up for me. What you're saying comes as a shock. A real surprise. He never mentioned bumping into the Nordstroms, probably because..." and I stopped.

"Because?" Everbright asked.

"Because." I swallowed hard. Then I figured, *What the heck?* I didn't have much pride left. George was in a tough spot. He'd yelled at Sven when he nearly hit Anya, and then he'd gotten into it with our neighbor at Antonio's. If I told Everbright what I suspected, at least he would understand why George had kept the news about the public scene from me. If I didn't share my reasoning, George would look more culpable. "I think my husband is cheating on me. According to him, he's out late with business meetings, but I know better. He didn't tell me about bumping into the Nordstroms, because he didn't want to explain why he was at a nice restaurant, when he was supposed to be working late at his office."

The skillet had heated nicely. I put the sandwich on, and, while it toasted, I made a fresh pot of coffee for Everbright. The kitchen seemed much more cheery with the rich fragrance of toasted cheese and the robust smell of brewing coffee.

"Okay." Everbright sounded convinced. Not happy. Not sad, but as though he was more sure that George had gotten in Sven's face—and as if he could see how a cheating husband might have plucked up the courage to at least stand up for his long-suffering wife. "I'll never understand some men. Why Mr. Lowenstein would..."

He stopped. "It's none of my business, but I think he's a lucky man to have you and his daughter."

The heat of a blush crept up my neck, and I was grateful he couldn't see my embarrassment, as I bent over the skillet and flipped over the sandwich. "That's very nice of you to say, but I don't think George feels that way all the time. Mainly he does, but there's a part of him —"

I bit my lip. This wasn't the time or place to share such a personal problem. Instead, I changed the direction of the conversation as I plated the food. "When you say that George nearly got into a fight with Sven, you aren't suggesting that George is responsible for Sven's death, are you? Because if you are, that's stupid. George wasn't here when Sven fell, and I called 911."

"We'll know more about Mr. Nordstrom's death once the lab

reports come in and we can analyze them." Everbright fell on the grilled cheese with gusto, gobbling it down in haste and, belatedly, realizing he hadn't thanked me. "Thanks," he managed between bites, while I prepared a second sandwich without asking, and poured him a cup of fresh coffee.

"Okay, you've made your point about needing more information." I put the second sandwich in the skillet and set a plate of cookies on the table. "But if the cause of Sven Nordstrom's death was the sloshing around of his brain, how could George or anyone else be responsible? George wasn't around, when it happened. Nobody was around. If I hadn't chosen that very minute to make a run to Home Depot, I wouldn't have seen Sven take his tumble either. Sven would have died all alone in his front yard."

"You don't have to be standing over a person to kill him." Everbright spoke so softly that I barely heard him.

I whirled around to face the detective. His mouth was shiny with the butter I'd used on the grilled cheese, and that slick surface somehow made him more transparent. He was studying me intensely, trying to measure my reactions to our conversation. "Are you suggesting that *I* did something to knock Sven off his bike? If so, why would I call an ambulance? Wouldn't I have left him there on the ground? Is that your point? Or are you saying it's my fault Sven and George got into a fight? That they fought because I wasn't getting along with the Nordstroms? Are you suggesting that I'm the one who caused Sven's death?"

Everbright pushed away his plate. While studying it, he rocked back in the chair, balancing it on two legs. I wasn't happy about that. It looked to me like he could go over backward any minute. "Actually, no. I'm simply trying to find out how deep the rift was between Nordstrom and your husband."

"Look, George didn't hurt Sven. That's not his style. I didn't either, and I was there when the man fell. As you might have noticed, I have my hands full with my kid and this mess. And George isn't stupid. Why would he fight with Sven in public and then kill him? For what? Because Sven was rude to me? Because he rode his bicycle too close to our daughter? Come on. That's just silly. You must have bigger fish to fry."

Everbright got up and took his dish to the sink.

I was on a roll. "No way would I have run out in front of Sven that morning and caused him to fall. If he had hit me, what would have become of Anya?"

Everbright reached into the cupboard and grabbed an empty glass. He stuck it under the facet and poured himself some water. "I hope you don't mind," he said, raising his drink to me in a questioning gesture.

"Of course not." His socks showed at the hem of his pants. His shoes needed a good shine. A button hung by threads from his shirt. But his eyes were intelligent, and they took in every detail of my expression. He studied me like I was a physics textbook and this was final exam day.

"Good point about your daughter," he said after he drained the glass.

"If I didn't do it and George didn't do it, who did? You're suggesting that Sven was either startled into falling or that he lost his balance because..." I hesitated while I sifted through the possibilities. "Because he'd been given or he'd taken a substance that caused him to lose his balance and fall off his bike that morning."

Everbright nodded, poured himself more water, and asked to use our bathroom.

While he was gone, I scrubbed the frying pan, dried it, and put it under the stove. Those iced cookies from Kaldi's were calling my name. Out of the initial dozen, only two were left. I helped myself to the smaller one. The first bite of sugar hit me with a jolt. Mentally, I could trace the sweetness as it flowed through my mouth, down my throat, into my tummy, and from there it spread magical energy to every cell in my body.

A sip of coffee offered the perfect accompaniment for the sugar, butter, and vanilla treat. The caffeine hit me — and with it came a sudden clarity.

As Everbright returned to the kitchen, I faced him down. "You keep telling me you haven't come to any conclusions, but that's not true, is it? You're pretty sure that Nordstrom was murdered. You've purposely avoided using that word — murdered — but that's the long and short of it. You came here today to rattle our cages, George's and mine. The point is that one or the other of us caused Sven to hit his head and die. That George and I are responsible. You blame us for our neighbor's death!"

He spread his hands in a placating way. "I have to consider every possibility. That's my job. I am paid to think the worst of people."

Because he was so matter-of-fact, I couldn't stay angry. What he said made sense; I couldn't argue the point. He had a job to do. My feelings weren't part of the calculation.

But I did need more clarity on another point. "The other possibility, the one you *haven't* mentioned, is that there's a cold-blooded murderer out there somewhere. Maybe even living in this neighborhood. Certainly in the metro-St. Louis area. And this creep is a planner, a person who arranged this particular situation, so it would look like an accident, but Sven would definitely die. Had I not been home that day or not walked outside when I did, Sven Nordstrom would have expired right there on his lawn. We're talking about a killer who's methodical, organized, and cool-headed."

"All true. If that's the case, the person I'm looking for is very dangerous. All killers are, but this jerk doesn't act impulsively, which means he's less likely to make a mistake. That'll make him — or her — harder to catch."

"Then I'm in danger. So is my daughter. When were you planning to tell me that?" Anger heated my face. "You came here today hoping to pin this on my husband. Or on me. Did you appoint yourself as judge and jury? What about protecting us? Isn't that part of your job?"

"If I thought you were in real danger, I would tell you. Usually crimes like this are perpetrated by the victim's nearest and dearest. Or a person with a reason to be angry. Maybe a conflict at work that escalated. Things of that nature. Consequently, I don't think you're in any danger at all. In fact, I'll make you a promise. If I hear anything that leads me to believe you are at risk, I'll give you a call immediately."

Picking up one of Anya's toys where it had fallen under the table, I studied it. "I'm not sure that's good enough."

"It has to be. Meanwhile, you need to be vigilant. Seeing that your husband is rarely home, taking extra precautions would be sensible. Keep your doors locked. Carry your cell phone with you at all times. Keep it charged. Report any suspicious behavior to us. Don't linger in your car, particularly with the doors unlocked."

All those suggestions frightened me, and my face must have shown my emotions.

"How's that for keeping you safe?" he added.

"That's...fine."

But it wasn't. Not really.

46

When Everbright left, I shut the door behind him, hard. I was that glad to see him go. Once I turned the lock, I bolted up the stairs, with my heart in my throat. I badly needed to see Anya, sleeping in her crib. I needed to know she was all right. I needed to remember what was at stake in our lives.

The sound of the front door slamming had awakened her from her nap. Those blue eyes blinked rapidly, taking in the world. While she came to her senses, I leaned over her and rubbed her back. She took a deep breath, signaling she was now alert.

"Mama?" She smiled at me. Seeing my daughter's sweet face cheered me — and, just as fast, it plunged me into a spiral of fear. Who had killed Sven Nordstrom? Why was that detective trying to pin it on George and me?

While I changed Anya, I went over my conversation with Everbright. Was he seriously suggesting that George was to blame? Or had he done it to see my reaction? Was it possible he'd given me fair warning, and my husband was being framed for murder?

As I taped on her diaper, Anya tried to squirm away. We seriously needed to start potty-training. But that would be impossible, if I couldn't clear a path to our toilets. Mert had told me she would get here as soon as possible. In the meantime, I needed to buckle down to the serious business of opening boxes and putting the contents away. Keeping busy would help me forget what I'd heard from Everbright.

Right. Like I was going to forget that a killer might be running around in our neighborhood! I laughed out loud at the absurdity of that.

Anya laughed, too, although fortunately, she didn't know what had struck me as funny.

If Everbright did suspect my husband, what should I do? I could phone George and warn him. Knowing George, he would laugh and ignore my message. Besides, did I really want to have a conversation like this with him over the phone? What if someone in his office overheard?

Another voice in my head piped up. George had been lying to me about his late night work sessions. My instincts had been on target, when I thought he acted guilty. Now I knew he'd been sneaking around. Dinner with another couple? If it had been a business meal, why would my husband have left his clients and spoken harshly to our neighbor?

The answer was: He wouldn't have.

George must have had a drink before he spouted off — and he must have felt at ease enough with his dinner companions that he was willing to put aside his manners and pick a fight with Sven Nordstrom. That meant he knew those dinner companions well.

And I knew, or rather I admitted to myself, George was stepping out on me. I couldn't avoid the truth any longer. But I could push it to the bottom of my worry list.

More importantly I needed to focus on keeping Anya safe.

Everbright had warned me to be vigilant. His warning came as an indirect admission there might be a killer loose in our neighborhood.

Dry, clean, and sweet smelling, Anya was now happy and wide awake. "Eat," she said.

"You're hungry, aren't you?" I picked her up, handed her a stuffed toy, and carefully carried her down the stairs.

Along the way, Anya chattered to Blue Bunny. My daughter's innocence and her trust in me hammered home my worst fears. To protect her, I had to protect her father, George. And I vowed that I would. Even if he wasn't being faithful to me, I couldn't let him go to jail for a crime he hadn't committed. On the other hand, it was hard to feel trust, when my spouse was actively lying to me.

Was it remotely possible he had done something to hurt Sven? Maybe something that had gone horribly wrong? Could George have killed Sven, accidently? If so, how? Sven hadn't died on the spot. It wasn't like he'd been shot and dropped to the ground.

Nevertheless, a cold and calculating killer had targeted Sven Nordstrom and had been successful in cutting his life short. Would he or she be successful in evading capture?

My head hurt. Once downstairs, I put Anya in her high chair. When she was strapped in, I grabbed a couple of Advil from the overhead cabinet. Sticking my head under the faucet in the sink, I swallowed them. They left a bad taste in my mouth.

Of course, almost everything in my life was leaving a bad taste in my mouth. I was choking on my husband's lies, the visits from the homicide detective, the mess that was my house, and my loneliness.

The doorbell rang.

"Doh," Anya said, and she pointed to our foyer.

"Right." The last shockwave to hit my house of cards would

be another visit from law enforcement. Even worse, what if a killer stood on my doorstep? My teeth began to chatter.

"Doh! Doh!" Anya pointed with her whole body.

I grabbed the box of Cheerios, put a handful on her tray, and left her pawing through them, while I went to take a look through the peep hole.

There stood Sheila. For once, I was glad to see her.

47

Sheila being Sheila, I couldn't get a word in edge-wise. Her habit of talking without accounting for her audience could be annoying. However, today I found it oddly comforting. She went on and on, covering in detail her irritation about Linnea needing a day off, her problems with one of the women at the country club, a strange noise coming from the engine of her Mercedes Benz, and her disappointment that George had been scarce lately.

As was also her habit, she plucked Anya from my arms without saying hello or asking permission. In fact, she never asked, "Is this a good time?" before she barreled into my life, like a runaway ox cart. I'd learned to wait her out. Eventually, she would wind down, and when she did, I would speak up on those rare occasions that I had anything to say for myself.

Stalking past me, Sheila carried Anya into the kitchen and eased down onto a chair, the same seat that Everbright had recently vacated.

"What on earth is George doing? How can he possibly be so busy? Of course, I know I'll see him for Friday night Shabbas. We're having it here, because Linnea insists on visiting her brother just because he's had a heart attack. Can you imagine? What did she expect? He was overweight, didn't exercise, and ate like a horse. Yet she mopes around all teary-eyed. Poppycock. She knows I can't do without her, but she is adamant that she take the train up to Chicago and see him."

As Sheila paused long enough to unclip an earring, rather than let Anya yank it from her earlobe, I managed to slip in the odd phrase calculated to get her attention. "A cop came by. He thinks George murdered our neighbor."

"What?" Sheila dropped the earring and nearly let Anya do a backward flip out of her arms. "What? I could not have heard you right. Repeat what you just said."

"Okay, but let me get Anya's lunch started."

Once again, I dragged out the skillet and cooked up a grilled cheese sandwich. This time, after letting it cool and tearing it into small pieces, I fed it to my daughter.

Sheila would never eat a grilled cheese sandwich. She has coffee for breakfast, salad for lunch, and a lean meat with veggies for dinner. The scant amount of flesh on her bones is testimony to her alcohol consumption, which seems to be considerable and frequent. Without asking, I poured her a cup of coffee. While she sipped it, I slapped together a grilled cheese for myself and told Sheila about the visit from Everbright. To her credit and my surprise, she listened carefully, not bothering to interrupt. When I explained about George getting into a public argument with Sven at Antonio's, Sheila *did* stop my narrative, quickly waving away any hint of impropriety. "Yes, yes. A working dinner, I'm sure. He's closing a big deal, a lot of parties involved. Wining and dining clients is part of his job."

"Uh-huh. Anyway, he couldn't or wouldn't tell me a lot. His excuse was that the lab hasn't processed all the evidence they've collected from the site. I guess it's not like on TV, when they get answers right away. But I have to tell you, Sheila, I'm scared."

"How dare you suggest that George was involved?"

"That is *not* what I said. Don't you dare misquote me." I slapped my grilled cheese sandwich onto a plate. "You are being totally unfair, Sheila. I defended George to the hilt, even though I had no idea he wasn't at his office all night the evening he went to Antonio's. I stuck up for George, I totally did, but it might not have made one iota of difference. I don't believe Everbright thinks I'm credible. He even hinted that I could be the guilty party."

"What on earth? How totally unprofessional of him! I have half a mind to call an attorney and sue him for libel."

"Slander," I said. "Libel is printed word; slander is spoken. Everbright's comment doesn't qualify for either. Just so you know."

"Whatever. He has no right to toss around accusations. What sort of person makes comments like that? It's irresponsible. He needs to be more careful about people's reputations. Just thinking about what that man said about George makes me furious."

I noticed she didn't seem upset about him blaming me for murder. But, then, I wasn't her child, and George was her son, her little boy. Since having Anya, I understood better how motherhood changed your world view. I saw everything in relationship to my daughter. Would it hurt her or help her? She was the lens through which I interpreted my life. And when you sat back and thought about it that made sense. If we didn't care for our children with every atom of our strength, how could they survive? Anya was incapable of doing for herself. I had to be her champion.

"It was your responsibility to set that awful man straight," Sheila interrupted my thoughts. "Why on earth did you even let him into your house? And talk to him? So what if George ate at Antonio's? My son is a businessman. He has meetings with clients, when they're available, not at his convenience. Why didn't you say that to Everbright? You should have explained that to the policeman and helped him to see that George's behavior was perfectly normal. Don't you have any sense? You should have told that man you weren't going to say anything without an attorney. Nothing! And when he started talking about George, you should have terminated the interview immediately."

"Detective Everbright told me he was collecting information; that's all. Look, Sheila, if I hadn't talked to him, I wouldn't have known they're probably investigating a murder. Then where would I be? So, sure, I'm worried about him blaming George, but I'm even more concerned that there's a cold-blooded killer on the loose in our neighborhood. George didn't kill Sven Nordstrom, but somebody did. Who's the guilty party? What if he strikes again? Think about it. I'm here all alone with Anya, most of the time! We could be at risk! How can I protect my baby?"

The tears I'd held back now flowed freely. Anya stared up from her tray, and her lower lip trembled. "Mama?" She looked semi-comical, with a yellow dribble of cheese stuck to her chin.

"Mama is fine, honey." I smiled at my daughter and flicked away tears that trailed down my face.

"I'm here, too, darling." Sheila leaned over to plant a kiss on Anya's head.

All the haughty anger had drained from my mother-in-law's face. Those blue eyes that had crackled with fury now swam in a pool of silvery tears. With a brisk wipe of the back of her hand, she knocked them aside. Sitting straighter in her chair, she squared her shoulders. "I am not about to let my family get hurt. Mark my words. No one is going to lay a hand on my granddaughter. We'll get this solved — and get it done quickly. I know just the man to call."

"Who?" I tore off a piece of paper toweling and dabbed my eyes. Anya went back to picking at her sandwich.

"An old boyfriend of mine. A man well-placed in the St. Louis County Police Department. He's the assistant police chief right now. His name is Robbie Holmes."

48

The doorbell rang, cutting short any more conversation about Sheila's old beau. My mother-in-law and I froze, staring at each other, hearing the echo of the ring, and silently wondering if murderers introduced themselves with such propriety.

"Doh?" Anya pointed helpfully in the right direction.

The bell rang again; this time more insistently.

"You stay with Anya," I told Sheila. "I'll go see what's up. Do you have your cell phone?"

She raised it and flashed it at me.

"Good. I'll holler, if you need to dial 911."

"Wait." Sheila stood up, walked away from the table, and reached into my knife block sitting on my counter. That bulky wooden object had been inside the first box I'd unpacked that was labeled KITCHEN. While Anya and I watched, Sheila pulled out the biggest cleaver I owned, a wedding gift that I'd thought strangely inappropriate at the time. Brandishing the weapon, she said, "Now you can answer the door."

Being armed and dangerous seemed perfectly logical under

the circumstances. I reached past Sheila to grab a paring knife. "Good thinking. This ought to slow him down."

"Yes." Sheila's eyes held an incredibly scary glint.

Anya paused while finger-painting her tray with the last of her grilled cheese sandwich. Her eyes traveled from her grandmother to me and back again. "Doh?" she asked hopefully.

Hiding the knife against my leg, I forced myself to walk through the short hallway and into the foyer. On tiptoes, I looked out the peephole. My vision was blocked by a heavily mascaraed eyeball staring back at me. It blinked and a voice said, "Kiki? You okay in there?"

It was Mert. I opened the door and fell into her arms. She hugged me back. When she stepped away, she spotted the knife I gripped in my right hand.

"Holy-moly. Have you lost your mind?" All her earrings shook, as she recoiled from me.

"Nope. Come on into the kitchen. I'll tell you what's happening."

I introduced Mert to Sheila. Of course, Anya needed no introduction, and she crowed with happiness at seeing her favorite bracelet donor.

"I had a break between jobs, and I figgered I'd come by here and see what I could get done," Mert said. "At least, I can give you an estimate. At best, I could help you rearrange these boxes so you've got space to move around. If this ain't a good time, I can leave."

"No, no, you're fine. Can I get you coffee or tea or lunch?"

"Nope. I ate on the way."

"If you two are going to tackle cleaning up, why don't I take Anya home with me? She'll be safe at my house." Sheila put a proprietary hand on my child's shoulder.

Actually, that was a great idea. Without Anya underfoot, Mert and I could make real progress. "Sure," I said, stuffing the paring knife into my back pocket. "Let me get her changed and cleaned up."

We were outside, loading Anya into Sheila's Mercedes Benz, when a plane flew overhead.

"Bird!" said Anya, pointing to the sky. The crisp fall weather put an extra touch of pink in her chubby cheeks.

"Airplane." I corrected her gently, as I buckled her car seat.

I backed my way out of the Mercedes. My maneuver left me facing the Nordstroms' garage. To my surprise, the door rolled up, all by itself.

"That is so weird," I muttered to myself.

49

When I closed and locked the front door behind us, I discovered that Mert had already begun dragging boxes to the far corners of the living room. "I can't stay for long, but I figured that even an hour or two could be enough to make progress. Here's what I'm thinking: This here formal living room is probably the room you use the least. If we can get these boxes rounded up, it'll free up space. If they're all piled up neatly, it'll be easier to clean around them."

The wisdom of her approach was immediately apparent. I picked up a small box and set it on top of the stack she'd started.

"You planning on using that there knife to open these?" Mert asked.

I'd forgotten about the paring knife in my back pocket. "No, I wasn't intending to use it on boxes. I grabbed it for protection. Give me a minute and I'll explain."

After I put the knife back in its place in the kitchen, I told Mert about Detective Everbright's visit. As I related the events, we worked together, pushing and shoving boxes.

"Poison. That has to be how the killer got rid of your neighbor." Mert turned a box so that the label faced out, making it easy to read. "Do you know that most poisoners never get caught? It's only when they commit one murder after another that they tip their hand."

I did not know that. "How come?"

Mert explained that autopsies don't test for every substance. "Besides, anything can be poison. See, it's all about the victim's health, weight, and other extenuating factors. For example, you can't poison a person with cheese and wine, exceptin' if that person is taking MAO inhibitors. Then the cheese and wine could be lethal."

"What's an MAO inhibitor?" We had moved to the kitchen. With two people unboxing, I could actually see progress.

"A type of antidepressant. My point is if you know what a person is taking for medications, you can do a lot of harm. You don't even need to feed 'em something weird. Here's another example, nicotine patches. Say a person is already chewing the nicotine gum and you cover their body in nicotine patches. Kaboom! They'd keel over."

"Mert, how come you know all this?"

She laughed. "I love those true crime programs on TV. And them books about real killers? I like mysteries, too. The puzzles in 'em really tickle me. Keeps me from thinking too much about real life, you know?"

"You're suggesting that Sven was poisoned. How?"

"I don't know," she said, "'cause I don't know enough about him."

"Hmmm."

"But I do know a thing or two about cops." She sounded bitter. "You shouldn't have talked to that detective. Not even to say a peep. Them cops'll twist and turn what you say. They'll use it against you. When cops sink their teeth into you, they work overtime to prove they're right. They can plant evidence. They can intimidate people into saying you was someplace when you weren't. They can put together a story that'll have you in jail faster than you can say, *What on God's green earth?*"

"I guess I shouldn't have let him in, huh?" I swallowed hard.

Belatedly, I realized that I probably should have been more careful about what I told her. I hadn't checked her references. I didn't know Mert other than our fateful meeting in Home Depot. Okay, I knew she cleaned for the Nordstroms, and it was entirely possible that she and they were great friends. But it was also possible they didn't like her. In fact, maybe they planned to fire her.

I had no way of knowing.

Suddenly the world wobbled. I felt light-headed. *Calm down,* I told myself. *Listen to your gut.*

I wanted Mert as a friend. Her down-home way of seeing the world, her plain-spoken style of communication, and her lack of pretense appealed to me. Obviously, she had a great deal of life experience. Mert was what my nana would have called "a smart cookie."

On the other hand, she also might have her own agenda. Going forward, I would limit our conversations to chitchat.

Trust would have to come later, when she proved herself.

50

*A*fter Mert left, Sheila surprised me. George must have given her a key, because she didn't ring or knock. There was the sound of the tumblers scraping and – *Poof!* – she appeared in the foyer with Anya.

My mother-in-law's sudden presence sent my heart into another round of fast-paced pounding. If she realized I was in a panic, she ignored my plight.

I, on the other hand, quickly realized that she was in a state. Nervous energy buzzed around her. Her eyes darted from corner to corner of the foyer, but wouldn't meet mine. She jiggled and bounced, keeping poor Anya off-balance in her arms.

"I totally forgot that I have a nail appointment. I would cancel, but I've had to reschedule three times in the past month. If I don't go this time, they won't let me make any more appointments. I have to get my nails done, before I have coffee with Robbie Holmes."

I couldn't see any link between having coffee with the assistant police chief and having polished nails, but I knew better than to argue with Sheila. Especially when she wore such a cloud of amped-up electricity. This was not the time to trifle with her.

"No problem. Mert and I actually got a lot done. She was only here two hours, but she helped me figure out a line of attack."

"Good." She handed Anya to me. "Glad to hear that woman could help, because you really do need to get this house picked up. If you weren't living in such a mess, George could bring his clients here to eat."

The accusation blindsided me. As soon as it was out of her mouth, she looked away. I'm not good at math, but I quickly put two and two together and came up with Catch-22. Sheila must have phoned George, asked him about his meal at Antonio's, and found a way to lay the blame at my feet. My blood boiled at her sneaky finger-pointing. George's misbehavior was all my fault? A housekeeping failure had encouraged him to cheat on me?

There had been countless nights back in our small, but organized, apartment, when he hadn't come home until the dawn's early light. Even if our home was a mess, why couldn't he ask me to join him for a meal with clients? Was I that much of a source of shame? If so, why had he married me? He had no right to be ashamed of me. My family came over before the Mayflower; we had a long and storied history. I had been an A student in college, until I got pregnant. There was no reason on earth that I should hang my head in shame. *None.*

"Right," I said, through clenched teeth. I didn't feel like fighting with Sheila. She would always protect her son.

Okay, yes, our house was a mess, but that didn't explain why George had never said to me, "Hey, Kiki, I'd like to introduce you to my friends that I grew up with." He'd kept me tucked away, like a dirty little secret.

As the heat rose in my face, Sheila turned her attention to

fussing with her cell phone. From the mumbles, I understood she was trying to call the nail salon. When she did, she explained she might be running a little late, because there'd been a family emergency. "My daughter-in-law begged me to take her baby off her hands. Yes, again. I've warned her she shouldn't stay up all night. Babies get up early. I'll be there as soon as I can."

She ended the call and gave me a sheepish smile.

My jaw was hanging open. I was angrier than I'd ever been. In fact, I could barely see for the haze of fury that descended on me. Without another word, I walked past her and carried Anya upstairs.

The bald truth of the matter was: Why should I worry about protecting George Lowenstein? He had his mother and his friends. He also had an active social life that excluded me. I was all alone in this world, except for my daughter. To protect her, I had to protect myself. I could not let myself be blamed for Sheila's chronic lateness, for George's infidelity, and possibly Sven Nordstrom's death.

As I lowered my daughter onto the changing table, I decided not to go back downstairs and see Sheila to the door. She let herself in; she could let herself out. Instead, I allowed myself the luxury of a long, sloppy cry. Anya played quietly in her crib.

When I was done, I washed my face with cold water and made a promise to the girl in the mirror. "I will not let these people defeat me. I will not let them treat me like a doormat. I will find a way to prove them wrong and to make them respect me. I'll do it for myself and for Anya. She deserves a mother who isn't a loser."

51

*A*nya had fallen asleep. I decided not to wake her.

After checking that Sheila had left, and that my front door was locked securely, I went back upstairs to look in on Anya. She looked like an angel, slumbering quietly.

Feeling the need for companionship, even if it was from a sleeping toddler, I lay down on the bed in her room. The physical labor from moving boxes put a pleasant ache in my limbs. With the emotional emptiness that follows a good cry, I fell asleep in minutes. I woke up feeling groggy, not refreshed, but the sound of Anya's happy gurgling reminded me of my vow. I would not let the cops or Sheila or George run over me. I would stand up for myself.

While I changed Anya, she pointed to the window. "Ou? Kitty? Wauk?"

"Of course we can take a walk, sweetheart. You want to see that kitty again, don't you? His name is Bartholomew. That's sort of a joke, you see, because 'mew' is a sound that a kitten makes. Mr. Bergen called him Bart. Can you say Bart?"

"Ba."

"Good enough."

Such balmy temperatures wouldn't last for long. Determined to take advantage of them, I dressed Anya in a sweater and hat.

The crisp leaves crunched beneath our feet on our first lap around the neighborhood. The second lap came to an abrupt halt, when I noticed a gray-haired woman withdrawing the mail from the Nordstroms' mailbox. At her side was a big black Labrador with soulful brown eyes.

"Doh!" Anya nearly lurched out of her stroller. "Doh! Woof!"

The woman responded to Anya's excited cries by smiling and grabbing her dog by the collar.

"May she pet the dog?" I asked, while keeping a respectful distance away.

"Yes, of course. Zoe loves children."

"Remember, be gentle," I said to Anya, after pushing the stroller close enough for Anya to reach out and pat the beautiful animal. I squatted down to monitor the way my child stroked the dog's fur. We had worked on this, although we didn't have a pet and had used stuffed animals for practicing. I was gratified to see how Anya remembered her lessons.

Zoe sat patiently, accepting the clumsy pats, and finally giving Anya a big, wet kiss that caused a fit of giggles.

I rose and extended a hand to the dog's owner. "Hi. I live across the street. I was very sorry to hear about Sven. My name's Kiki Lowenstein. This is Anya. My husband is George."

"Brita Morgenstern." Her rough hand intercepted mine and gave it a brisk shake. Brita's fine lines and wrinkles suggested she was in her late sixties. Salt-and-pepper hair was gradually being overtaken by white and silver strands. Although she was taller than I, she wasn't as tall as her brother. A slight hump in her back put us nearly at eye level.

"Sven was my half-brother. Nearly twenty years my junior; the product of a second marriage by my father to a much younger woman. I never expected him to die before me. I must admit that it's a bit surreal."

"I imagine. Would you like to come over for a cup of tea? I have some fresh muffins from Dierbergs. They're lemon poppy seed. I think Anya's had enough of being outside for one day." I pointed to my child and her runny nose, while I prepared for Brita's rejection.

Surprisingly, the older woman smiled. "Sure. I would like that, but I need to set down all this mail and get Zoe's leash. Would you care to step inside?"

Since I'd never been a guest in the Nordstroms' home, I accepted the invitation on the spot. I liked Brita immediately. The lumpy sweater she wore had been created with a variety of yarns, giving it a patchwork flavor. Her mom-jeans were well-worn. Everything about this woman shouted, "I know who I am and I am comfortable with myself." She radiated a sense of acceptance, the sort of comfortable feeling you get when you've been friends with someone for years.

While Brita led the way, I pushed the stroller toward the house. Zoe trotted along at the woman's side, as if tethered by an invisible leash.

"How old is Anya?" Brita asked as she pushed open the door.

"Two years and four months."

I lifted Anya and the stroller up and onto the stoop. Brita stepped inside and held the door open. The change from the brightly lit outside and the dim interior momentarily blinded me. When I could see again, I gasped with astonishment.

My first impression was a snow bank. The place had been decorated in white, white, and white, with white accents. Gold and crystal sparkled everywhere, blinding me. In fact, if it were possible to fall headfirst into a tub of white glitter, this might be the outcome.

As I took in my surroundings, my eyes came to rest on a huge portrait hanging over the white brick fireplace. By huge, I mean life-size, although it seemed even larger, because of the subject matter and the positioning of the piece.

Staring down on me with a haughty look on her face, was the full-frontal, stark-naked Leesa Nordstrom, leaning against a pure white marble column. The pose was arresting, provocative even. Coupled with the subject matter, it was doubly so. Leesa's cornflower blue eyes, the white-blonde hair, her in-your-face sensuality and nudity were nearly overpowering. I couldn't think of anything appropriate to say. Not one word. Instead, I gaped. I stared. Finally, I shook my head as if to break the trance I was in.

"Rather hard to take, isn't it? Leesa insisted on hanging it here. Sven objected strenuously. She called him a prude. He called her, well, it isn't worth repeating. Not now, anyway." Brita reached into a wooden bowl and removed a red dog's leash. Zoe obediently walked over and sat at her feet.

"Wow. I wouldn't think him prudish. It's just a bit, uh, over-the-top for a living room. At least, that's my humble opinion."

"Mine as well." Brita hesitated before snapping on the leash. "I should have asked. Would you prefer that I leave Zoe at home?"

"No, please bring her. She's very welcome to come. Anya would love that. I would too. I love animals."

"Good," Brita said. "That means we're going to be good friends. I can feel it."

52

---

*A*nya giggled from her comfortable spot in Brita's lap. Zoe had lowered herself to the floor with a groan and promptly fallen asleep.

"My poor dog is a senior citizen," Brita said, noticing that I'd reacted to Zoe's groan. "She's an English Lab. I adopted her when she was just a pup. There were nine in her litter. When I got her home, I discovered she only has four toes on one paw. I mentioned it to the breeder, and she offered to exchange Zoe for a dog with all the usual toes, but I couldn't do that. I'd already fallen in love with her. She's such a loving animal. She's good with people, other dogs, cats, rabbits, squirrels, and even chipmunks."

Anya peered over Brita's knee at Zoe. "Doh. Good doh."

"Yes, sweetie," I assured her. "Zoe is a very good dog."

The timer dinged, and I took the lemon poppy seed muffins out of my microwave oven. "I've never seen anything like that painting of Leesa."

"Nor has anyone else, I'd wager. How about you, Miss Anya? Did you like that silly painting? No. Me neither, darling."

"Doh?" Anya had mastered an all-purpose word. It could mean down, door, outdoors, dog, or even duh.

"Actually," I said. "I find Leesa's choice of home decor immensely cheering."

"How so?"

"My mother-in-law thinks poorly of me. If she got a gander at that painting, I believe she'd have a re-think."

"I imagine so. Tell me, do you get on with my sister-in-law? Was she nice to you?" Brita's blue-gray eyes shone with sincerity. I threw any last shreds of caution aside.

"Nope. She didn't like me from the git-go, as we say here in Missouri. Your brother didn't seem to care much for me, either."

Brita lifted Anya into her high chair. At first, I thought I'd offended the woman and she was preparing to go. However, once she settled Anya in, Brita pulled an embroidery hoop from a deep pocket of her sweater. With practiced skill, a silver needle flashed in and out of the muslin. "I'm not surprised. Saddened, but not surprised. My brother changed after his marriage. Leesa brought out the worst in him. One might think I am mourning now, since he died. But the truth is over the five years they were together, I lost my little brother a bit at a time. After he met Leesa, he became distant and moody. I am not surprised to hear you thought he didn't like you. I rather think he didn't like himself."

"Are you staying for the funeral?"

She glanced up and nodded. Her eyes were wet with unshed tears. "Although I don't know when that will be. They've asked to do a variety of tests on...the corpse. Leesa is totally opposed to it. She demanded that his body be cremated immediately. However, they won't release it. I think it's rather a good thing."

"Why?"

"Because I do not think, for one moment, that Sven died of natural causes."

"Then what do you think happened?"

"I think Leesa killed him."

As if responding the accusation, Anya tossed her empty sippy cup into the air. I dove for it, feeling happy about the distraction. If Leesa killed Sven, that meant I really *was* living next door to a murderer. Should I call the cops?

And, if I did, what would I say? My dead neighbor's half-sister suspects Leesa Nordstrom of killing Sven? Whoop-dee-do. That and a mushy Cheerio would have the same weight in their investigations.

Besides, after the warnings from Sheila and Mert, I knew I should avoid any more encounters with the cops. As unassuming as Everbright was, I also knew him to be smart and focused. Was it possible that I'd already told him too much?

"I said as much to the authorities, when they sent a detective around to chat with me. I told them that they should investigate Leesa. She's an evil, conniving woman."

"How did the detective respond? Was it Everbright that you spoke to?" I sat back down after giving Anya a refill of apple juice.

"Yes, that was the cop's name." Brita clasped the wooden embroidery hoop to her chest. "He said nothing when I told him to look more closely at Leesa. But why should he believe me? I am only a grieving sister. An out-of-towner sticking her nose in local business. My opinion matters little. What I need is evidence. Cold hard evidence."

"How do you propose to get that?"

"By going through the house. Inch by inch. Drawer by drawer. Leesa is not very bright, and she's totally self-absorbed. If she killed him, she might have taken notes on how. Or pulled up information on the computer. If she paid someone else to do it, there might be a suspicious phone number or a trail of money. Something that points to her involvement."

I told Brita about the argument that Sven and Leesa had in our driveway, the night of their party.

"In a Jaguar, you say? That's the car their guest was driving?"

"Yes. It was black. Looked new to me. The owner was about five-eight, in his late forties, thick black hair. Swarthy skin. Wore a knit shirt open to his belt. Gold chain."

"Larsen. Has to be. Lars Larsen. His real first name is Rudolph, but, because everyone here knows the reindeer song, he never uses it."

"Then you know him?"

Bending her head, she went back to her needlework. At first, I didn't think she heard me. But as I opened my mouth to repeat my question, Brita said, "Yes. I know him. We are..." and she stopped. Wiping her eyes with the back of her hand, she sipped her tea. When she composed herself, she said, "Rudolph is my son."

53

"To be absolutely accurate, Rudolph 'Lars' Larsen is my husband's son by his first marriage," Brita said. "I was a divorcée when his father, Big Lars, and I married. I didn't change my name because I had a career as a fiber artist."

Her fingers worked furiously, stabbing the fabric over and over with increasing intensity, "After Big Lars died, Rudolph lost his way in the world. His mother was never very good with him. He dropped out of school. Fell in with a bad crowd. He hated me, because I had been there by his father's side, when Big Lars was called to the Lord. Little Lars had been in a bar. We couldn't find him in time to get him word."

After a sip of her tea, she added, "I never tried to take his mother's place, but Lars thought I expected to. I guess he expected Big Lars to live out his years all alone. Or maybe he was upset to think that Big Lars would leave me money in his will. He didn't. I specifically told him not to. Whatever the reason, Lars has been purely hateful to me, from the moment we met."

I swung Anya down, dragged out a few plastic containers from a box, poured Cheerios in them, and let her play. She loved peeling off the lids, dumping the little O's and refilling the tubs again and again. "Lars lives here now? Surely he didn't drive down from Minnesota just for their party."

"Yes, Lars lives here. Sven didn't know until after he and Leesa moved to St. Louis. Leesa tricked my brother. She demanded that they move here. She claimed she had an old girlfriend from school who owned a modeling agency here. The plan was for Leesa to get away from Lars and make a new start. Instead, Leesa planned to isolate Sven. Take him away from family. She wanted to continue her 'career,' no matter what."

"Get away from Lars," I repeated. "Were he and Leesa having an affair?" That sounded crude, even to my ears, and I rushed to add, "Sorry if I spoke out of turn."

Brita's laugh was harsh. "There is no reason to apologize. None! Anyone might think that. It was not an affair. You see, no one could love Leesa as much as she loves herself. It was, however, an entanglement. Lars was part of that. Absolutely. Without a doubt."

She'd lost me. The key rested in the word "entanglement." What did she mean by that? I waited and she plunged ahead.

"Leesa was a porn star. Rudolph was her producer."

54

*A*s most stories begin, this one started quite innocently. Brita explained that Leesa Karlson was a gorgeous girl who turned heads and won a few local beauty contests in Sweden.

"Her parents moved to St. Paul, when she was a teen. Looking back, I suspect they had good reasons. Knowing Leesa, she was probably into mischief, in Stockholm, and they hoped that, by uprooting her, they could control her. But Leesa is willful and sneaky. Sven met her through a blind date. She had told the other girl that she was twenty. Of course, she was younger than that. Sven should have broken it off, when he learned she was fifteen. Instead, he courted her under her parents' watchful eye and married her a year later."

"What?" I sputtered. "She was only sixteen?"

"In Minnesota, you can marry at age sixteen with your parents' consent. Frankly, I think the Karlsons washed their hands of their daughter. They'd had enough. After she married, they moved back to Sweden."

"Wow." I couldn't imagine getting married at sixteen. Sure, I'd married young, but each year from thirteen to twenty is a huge leap. Although it's only 365 days chronologically, your maturation is much more than the sum of those months and weeks. It's an amazing time for personal growth.

"Leesa had Sven wrapped around her little finger," Brita said. "For their first anniversary, she decided to make a video. A sexy video, based on their most daring fantasies. Leesa wanted them to come to life for him."

That sounded perfectly plausible. I'd read about a photographer in St. Louis, who reportedly made a good living producing fantasy videos for couples. All involved parties signed contracts binding them to secrecy. Only one copy of the video was ever produced, and it was handed over to the purchasers.

Another photographer took "intimate" portraits. An article in the newspaper had profiled him. He was an ordinary man, looking for a niche market when he found one. His wife attended all his photo sessions. "It's strictly business," he said. "I focus on lighting, the pose, and getting a good product. Before this, I did still shots of food for ads."

In fact, as kinky as it sounded, a part of me thought, *Why not? Shouldn't people be entitled to privacy in their bedrooms and their personal lives?*

Just as quickly, I reversed my thinking. *Who would have the self-confidence or the nerve to strip down and act out her fantasies in front of a bright lights and a camera?*

I wouldn't. The dark was my best friend.

"Of course, Leesa needed someone to tape the session. A person with access to a video camera, tripod, and lights. Rudolph didn't have a job at the time. He's always been chronically underemployed. Lars loves porn, and he was family —" Brita added air quotation marks to this last word, "— so that would have been that if only this little escapade ended there. Well, it didn't. Leesa loved doing the shoot. The video actually turned out much better than she had expected. Rudolph had done a great job and stumbled onto his dream career. If only he could come up with the money to start a studio, he would be set. "

Zoe harrumphed and rolled to her feet. With a quiet whimper, she appealed to her mistress. Brita walked over to my back door, let the dog out and kept on talking. "Rudolph's teachers always complained that he didn't apply himself. That changed when he produced Leesa's video. Suddenly, he had done something that was remarkable."

"But the only people who would have seen that video were Leesa and Sven, right? Plus Rudolph, because he shot it."

"Yes. That's the way it was supposed to work. But, as it happened, copies of the video soon made their way onto the Internet. Sven found out when a co-worker showed him a screen shot."

"That must have been devastating."

"Leesa swears she never gave Rudolph permission. According to her, he sold the tape without her knowledge. She claimed to be every bit as shocked and upset as Sven was."

"Really?" From the little I knew of Leesa, I wouldn't have put anything past her. As the over-sized portrait in her living room proved, she harbored a streak of exhibitionism as broad and wide as the muddy Mississippi.

Brita opened the door, and Zoe trotted in. The dog sat obediently, while Brita wiped off her paws with a paper towel. "I don't believe it. I can tell you don't either. Sven wanted to believe it, but deep in his heart, he knew better. Suddenly, my brother found himself married to a porn star. Leesa swore that she was appalled. She said it would never happen again, but within a month, another video surfaced. And another. And another."

"How long has this been going on?"

"Three years. The move here was supposed to bring Leesa's career to an end. She promised Sven she would find work as a legitimate model and an exercise instructor." Brita slipped back into her chair. After sniffing Anya and receiving a piece of muffin for her troubles, Zoe again grunted her way into a prone position. This time, she rested her head on Brita's shoes. "Her promises meant nothing. Nothing! Sven told me last month that she'd begun filming again. I have no doubt that's why she was adamant about moving to St. Louis. She knew Rudolph was here, and she also knew that he had set up a studio."

55

*A*s I walked Brita and her dog to the front door, Anya burst into tears. "Doh! Doh!" she sobbed, throwing her weight at the retreating animal. Day by day, my daughter was becoming more and more of her own person with particular likes and dislikes. Her intense willpower often exhausted me. When she pulled this stunt — throwing her weight toward the object of her desire — I worried she would topple out of my grasp and hit the floor. Parenting a small child is largely a matter of keeping the kid alive.

To help Anya through the transition, we waited on the sidewalk, until Brita and Zoe disappeared inside the Nordstrom home. All the while, I assured my child that she'd see Zoe again. "Someday you'll have a dog of your own. I promise."

When we pivoted back toward our house, Anya yelled, "Bar! Ki!" she yelled, flailing her arms and pointing so that I'd see what she'd spotted, too.

Bartholomew, the Bergens' black cat, strolled out of the Nordstroms' garage. Once out in the open, Bart checked to make sure the coast was clear. Then he pitter-pattered across the street on soundless paws. His gaze fixated on the narrow strip of weeds that separated the edge of our property from the vacant lot next door.

Once he crossed the street, Bart's posture changed. Instead of head-down with quick steps, he crouched to a near crawl. His tail flicked left and right.

"Ki?" Anya watched with total absorption. "Mama? Ki?" She reached up to hook a finger into my mouth. With this fleshy bridle guiding me, I turned my head to follow her gaze. Bart was in full predator mode, low to the ground, his entire body coiled and ready.

Suddenly, he leaped forward and pounced on something in the tall grasses. Then he bounced along, zigzagging left and right, as he hunted his prey.

Anya was entranced. Her reaction brought a smile to my face. I love animals. There wasn't much I personally could give my daughter in terms of material goods, but I did hope I could instill in her my own sense of wonder at the natural world. While she crowed with delight at the miniature panther's antics, I cuddled her. But Anya didn't want a kiss. That would interrupt her immersion in the cat's pursuit. I gave her one anyway.

That's what we were doing, when Robbie Holmes pulled up in a marked police car. The gold and black lettering on the white cruiser announced he was part of the St. Louis County Police Department.

I hadn't met Robbie, but I'd seen him on TV. Sheila had pointed him out to me when he had appeared in the news. The man couldn't be mistaken for anyone else, because he was a dominating presence. At more than six feet tall, with the build of an ex-football player, and a full head of salt-and-pepper hair, Robbie was an attractive guy. Moreover, his easy smile instantly comforted me. Finally a law enforcement official who was definitely on our side.

"You must be Kiki." He extended his hand for a shake.

"Yes, and you must be Robbie Holmes. This is Anya." My daughter suddenly had a case of shyness. She buried her face in my shoulder. Robbie didn't push himself on her, and I respected him for that. Too often, adults force themselves on kids. No wonder children get abused and don't speak up. If we teach them that any adult has the right to invade their personal space, it's a short hop to accepting an inappropriate touch.

"I would have recognized Sheila's granddaughter anywhere. She has eyes the same color as her dad, doesn't she? And as Sheila has. What a beauty this little girl is going to be."

"Would you like to come in? The place is a bit of a mess, but you're welcome to a cup of coffee. I'm going to unpack a few more boxes, if Anya will sit quietly in her playpen."

"Lead the way." He held the door open for me. When I faltered a bit on the threshold, Robbie took me by the elbow as any gentleman would. There was a lot about Robbie that harked back to a time when people set great store by their manners.

"Terrific spot you have here. Once your grass comes in, and you get a few more trees planted, this will be very nice. Of course, this is some house. George did a nice job."

"Yes, he did. When I get all these boxes out of here, you'll really be able to see it to best advantage." I lowered Anya into her playpen. Immediately, she puckered up and whined.

"How about if I move her playpen closer to the kitchen?" Robbie asked. "I love kids. I can distract her, if you don't mind."

"Sure. That would be great."

After we got Anya situated, I poured Robbie coffee, started a third pot, and set out the last chocolate chip cookies I'd made. As he settled into his seat, I ripped the packing tape off yet another box. The fancy dishware inside would go on a top shelf. Since I'm only 5'3", I would need to stand on a chair. When I dragged one over, Robbie protested.

"Whoa. That's not safe. If you hand the things to me, I'll put them away. Will that work? You can tell me everything you know about your neighbors, the Nordstroms."

"That would be great."

Working in tandem, we made emptied the box. I rehashed our problems with Sven nearly hitting Anya and his vehement brush-off after his first fall. Robbie listened carefully when I explained about Mr. Colter's visit. He also paid attention as I went over what I saw happen during the Nordstroms' party. Once in a while, he would ask me for clarification. Otherwise, Robbie proved a good listener and a terrific helper to boot.

I told him what I'd recently learned from Brita. He brought over a box from the living room, opened it for me, and went back to retrieve a toy that Anya had tossed. Shaking his head, Robbie said, "There are a lot of avenues of inquiry. A lot of suspects. At least from what you've said. Does Everbright know about the porn?"

"Not from me. Brita Morgenstern ended her visit right before you pulled up. I haven't had a chance to tell Everbright what she said about Leesa's career in the sex industry."

I stood there with a couple of cookbooks in hand. "Is Everbright competent? He seemed to be focusing a lot on George. Is that fair? I shouldn't have told Everbright anything. I thought I was helping. If there's a murderer in our neighborhood, I want that creep locked up and behind bars. Anya and I are alone a lot of the time. I'm scared..." and my throat squeezed shut.

Without warning, tears threatened. "I'm being silly," I said, as I brushed at my eyes away.

"No, you're not." Robbie gave me a gentle grin. "You're a young mother with a child to protect. You have every reason to be worried. You look exhausted. There's no way you can unbox this mess by yourself."

"I hired a cleaning lady, Mert Chambers. She came over for an hour and a half between jobs. With two of us, we made real progress. But, by myself, I just can't....I don't seem to..." I stopped, rather than babble on and on.

"Do *you* think George was involved in Sven Nordstrom's murder?" Robbie spoke in the most matter-of-fact way possible, even though he was asking point-blank if I believed my husband was a murderer.

"Absolutely not! That's not like George. Okay, sure, George argued with Sven at Antonio's. But that's a far cry from getting violent or whatever. I don't even know how Sven died. One minute, he's out riding his bike, and the next, he's on the ground. I assume someone gave Sven Nordstrom something that took a while to work through his system. Whatever it was, I didn't do it, and George didn't either!" Leaning over the sink, I splashed a little cold water on my face.

"Okay. Got it." Robbie held up his hands in a gesture of surrender.

I felt angry, scared, and betrayed. "You can't seriously believe George or I were involved. What was our motive? Okay, they called the HOA on us, because our lawn is a mess. Big deal. George is looking into having sod laid. Sure, Sven rode his bike too near Anya and spooked her. She's not scarred for life, as you can well attest. Yes, they weren't nice to me when I took them gifts. Big whoop. I brought the chocolate cake and the flowers home with me. See? No harm, no foul. None of that matters."

"Sven was poisoned over time. The person who did it had ongoing access to him. The lab found George's fingerprints on Sven's bike."

"That's because Sven swerved too close to Anya and George grabbed at the bike."

"There's also the altercation at Antonio's. According to witnesses, your husband looked pretty upset."

"Hello? If you were slowly poisoning your neighbor to death, why would you make a scene in public? Why call attention to the fact you weren't getting along?"

Robbie rubbed his chin thoughtfully. "There is another little matter. It seems your husband knew Mrs. Nordstrom. Rather well, in fact."

56

"George knew Leesa? Are you kidding me?" The room swam before my eyes. If I hadn't been so close to the kitchen counter, I would have crumpled to the floor. As it was, Robbie jumped to his feet and grabbed me when my knees buckled.

"You better sit down." He pulled out a chair for me. As I cradled my face in my hands, he poured me a glass of water.

What was it with cops and glasses of water? *Sheesh.*

"Diet Dr Pepper." I pointed to the refrigerator. I needed the jolt of reality a caffeinated beverage would deliver. I had to be dreaming. This situation was getting worse by the minute. Not only was George cheating on me, he was messing around with a porn star? A porn star who was also our neighbor?

I heard the refrigerator door open and close. A cold can was slid in front of me. Robbie's voice seemed to come from far away. "According to Mrs. Nordstrom, your husband visited the studio where she works as a model. I don't think Everbright knew more about her, um, career than that. Mrs. Nordstrom claims that George was smitten with her. She claims he even stalked her."

"We live across the street! She accused me of the same thing when I took a class she taught. What's her problem? Does she seriously expect us to never cross her path? That woman has a lot of nerve." I popped the top on the can. The hiss of the bubbles promised a treat. I gulped it greedily. "You believe her?"

After retrieving another one of Anya's stuffed animals that she'd tossed over the side of her playpen, Robbie shook his head violently. "It's not my place to believe her or not. They let me read the files, because I'm the assistant police chief of St. Louis County. I didn't get the chance to ask Detective Everbright his opinion. As you can imagine, our overlapping jurisdictions complicate everything. All our 91 different municipalities protect their pieces of turf. Fortunately, we have a very cordial relationship between our department and Ladue, and the Ladue police chief is an old friend. I'm trusting you with this information, because Sheila and I have known each other for decades."

I took another gulp. "Then you're telling me that this was all in Everbright's police report. All this nonsense about George being a stalker?"

"Uh-huh." Robbie rose and poured himself a second cup of coffee. If cops kept visiting me, I'd need to make a run by Kaldi's and buy more beans.

And cookies. Lots and lots of iced cookies, muffins, and more slice-and-bake chocolate chip cookies, too.

Meanwhile Anya was happily playing in her playpen. She would pick up the various plastic shapes, one at a time, and stuff them into the shape sorter. She never got bored with this. Maria Montessori called it "purposeful play." What looked tedious was creating all sorts of important pathways in Anya's brain.

That was good news, because my brains were slowly getting fried. Each new day was bringing more and more stress to my life.

Robbie pulled a notebook from his jacket pocket. "Everbright says that a guy named Lars Larsen confirmed your husband's visit to the, uh, modeling studio."

"Rudolph 'Lars' Larsen is Brita Morgenstern's stepson," I said. "He produces porn in that studio; Leesa is his big star. Everbright should have also reported that I saw Leesa fighting with a man who must have been Lars. Just this morning I learned Sven wasn't happy about his wife being a porn star. They moved here to get Leesa away from that lifestyle, but she probably tricked Sven. She knew that Lars had built his studio in St. Louis. That means both Lars and Leesa with a motive for murdering Sven."

"Right. Like I said, there are a lot of avenues of inquiry." Robbie frowned. "Mrs. Nordstrom wasn't completely forthcoming about her line of work. Not initially, at least."

I blurted out, "I have to know: How much trouble is George in? They don't really suspect him of being a murderer, do they?"

Robbie turned sad eyes on me. "At this point, anyone and everyone is under suspicion."

57

Only after Robbie Holmes left did I realize he hadn't told me specifically what sort of poison Sven Nordstrom had ingested. Maybe he'd intentionally avoided sharing that specific information. Or maybe he didn't know. I couldn't tell. I had these sense that Robbie was a lot sharper than he seemed, just like Everbright was. Maybe that was a requirement for those wanting to enter law enforcement as a career. They had to seem unassuming, so they could trick people like me into talking too much.

And I probably had talked too much. But, then again, Sheila trusted Robbie Holmes. Surely that meant I should trust him, too.

Thinking back about what I'd learned, it was easy to see that George was in trouble, and a mean little voice inside me said, "He deserves it."

I'd imagined him with one woman, someone from his past. That would explain why he'd avoided introducing me to his old school chums. But had he also been unfaithful with Leesa? Was he a porn addict? A stalker?

There was a lot I didn't know about my husband. I thought I

knew his heart. I had let myself believe I knew what sort of man he was. Had I blinded myself, because I'd been eager to get married?

Hot tears prickled the back of my eyes. I pinched my nose, hoping not to cry. I rarely admitted to myself how eager I'd been to get away from my own family. My mother acted like she hated me. My father had too. Sure, I'd accidentally gotten pregnant, but how much of an accident had it really been? Was that the lie I told myself, so I wouldn't have to face the truth?

Was it possible that Anya would be raised by two liars? If that were the case, did I believe that George had nothing to do with Sven Nordstrom's death? Wasn't it remotely possible that George had killed him? My husband was adept at hiding things from me. He certainly had been careful to hide his involvement with Leesa Nordstrom. From the way he'd acted, I thought they hadn't met until we moved here.

Rubbing my temples, I made a decision. I would trust George. I had to. For Anya's sake. I would do everything I could to prove him innocent.

But if George didn't do it, who did?

If George didn't do it, a killer might be living right here in our neighborhood. How long would it be until the murderer struck again?

I had a daughter to protect, and a husband whose hours could best be defined as "erratic." If an intruder crept in, hours could go by before anyone knew I was in trouble. The weight of my isolation pressed down on me.

My phone rang, and I grabbed it up. Any noise that would drown out the frightened conversation in my head was sorely welcome. "Hello?"

"It's Mert. I'm calling to set a time for me to come and help you clean up that mess. You got a calendar?"

"I don't need a calendar. I have nothing to look forward to. Nothing!" A tiny sob leaked from me.

"Whoa. You okay?"

"No. Not really." I covered my mouth to suppress the noises, but my desperation had reached such a level that my gesture proved ineffective. I choked out a long, low sob. Anya dropped her red plastic triangle and stared at me.

"What are you doing right now?" Mert asked.

"Sitting here in my kitchen, staring at boxes, thinking about my last visitor, and trying not to get hysterical."

"You like pizza?"

"Who doesn't like pizza?"

"What do you like on yours?"

"I am not picky."

"Can you hang on until six? I'm on the other side of town."

"I think so."

"See you then."

58

*M*ert proved as good as her word. She arrived carrying a reusable wine bag. Inside were two bottles, white and red.

"Pizza should be here any minute." She pushed past me into my kitchen. "Smells like smoke in here."

I explained my mishap with the fireplace. "Can you believe a day has gone by, and this place still stinks?"

"I also smell burnt apples. How come?"

By the time I'd explained the entire fiasco, she was practically rolling on the floor with laughter. "Lord love you. You surely know how to get a man's attention. That there cop probably saw himself as a man with a white hat, riding in to rescue the fair maiden, for sure."

"Which one?" I asked.

"What do you mean?"

"I mean which cop are you talking about in the white hat? I've had two of them stop by."

"Lordy, you've been busy."

The wineglasses were still in a box somewhere, but two of Anya's sippy cups were clean and sitting in the drainer.

Mert pulled a corkscrew from her purse. With a deft couple of turns, she pulled out the cork and poured two hearty helpings. The fragrance of grapes on a hot summer day enveloped us.

"Here's to household calamities," I said as I lifted a sippy cup. "May they keep a smile on our faces."

After a long drink, Mert added, "And to dead neighbors. Thanks to Mr. Nordstrom biting the dust, my calendar has opened up so's I got plenty of time to help you out."

"Mert, those cops say Sven was murdered! That means a killer is on the streets. Maybe even living here in this very neighborhood!"

She pulled up a chair. Both earlobes sparkled with a parade of various earrings, from fake gems to hoops. Sequins decorated the deeply plunging neckline of her turquoise knit top. Her black jeans were skin-tight; rhinestones outlined the back pockets. Mert was a walking, talking light show, a veritable visual rainbow of fake gemstones.

"Look-it here, girl. You don't need more junk to worry about. You're letting your imagination run wild. There ain't no killers out there roaming your neighborhood. That ain't how it works."

Her explanation was interrupted by the doorbell. I felt my heart sink. Was yet another law official at the door?

"Don't panic none. The pizza's here," Mert said.

I hopped up; she followed.

"I've got this," I said. "You brought the wine, and I owe you for averting an ER visit."

After I paid and tipped the pizza delivery boy, I handed the box to her. Back in the kitchen, I found two paper plates. "I sure hope you don't eat your pizza off of good china with a knife and a fork. If you do, you're out of luck."

"Who eats pizza with a knife and fork? I never heard of such nonsense."

"My mother-in-law." My mouth watered at the smell of spicy sausage, rich tomato sauce, and tangy cheese.

"Huh. That woman acts like she has a corn cob up her you-know-where."

"If she does, it's gold-plated, and it came from Tiffany's."

That sent Mert into spasms of laughter.

"Girl, from the outside, it looks like you've got everything a woman could want. But I guess that's why they say appearances are deceiving, huh? Your world is definitely no picnic."

"You can say that again."

59

*A*n hour after Mert arrived, George called to say he'd be coming home late.

"Fine," I said and ended the call. Did it really matter?

Our marriage was a sham, and we both knew it.

But this wasn't the time for calling his bluff. I didn't have the mental or emotional energy to confront him.

"Tell me everything about this here murder case," she said. She and I plowed through the pizza and the first bottle of wine. Although I was well lubricated, I avoided telling her what I suspected about George's infidelity. I ended by explaining I was scared to death for our safety, mine and Anya's.

"You shouldn't be." She opened the second bottle.

I raised an eyebrow. "Why not?"

"Sven Nordstrom's death was probably done by someone with a grudge against him. Strangers don't murder other strangers like that. Once in a while there's a drive-by shooting or a robbery, but you gotta get real close to someone to keep giving him poison. Besides, poison is a woman's weapon of choice."

"Is it?"

"Yup. Remember *Arsenic and Old Lace?*"

"That's a play, right? Two little old ladies?"

"Uh-huh."

That led us to other subjects. My house. Her son, Roger. Raising kids. How she came to work for the Nordstroms, after they'd let another woman go, because she'd written bad checks on their account. Finding a hobby. Mert liked square-dancing and line-dancing. That sounded fun, but I'd grown up with ballet lessons. I was a bit of a dance snob, and this was the first time I'd recognized my prejudice.

We laughed about Mert's date with the guy from Home Depot. He turned out to be a sweet man but definitely not her type.

The evening passed by quickly. Adding to the pleasure of the wine and a listening ear was the sense I was making a real friend at last!

It was only after I'd said goodnight to Mert and climbed into bed that it struck me: She hadn't made one regretful reference to Sven Nordstrom. Not one single utterance of sadness. Nor had she commented on Leesa's grief.

That left me staring at the ceiling in Anya's room and thinking hard. Why didn't Mert seem to care about Sven's death? She didn't strike me as an unkind person. Her behavior toward Anya showed that Mert had tons of empathy. In fact, Anya had been so taken with Mert that she'd begged the woman to read her a bedtime story. Mert had kindly done that, repeating *Goodnight Moon* for a second and third time.

To me, Mert had been easy to get to know, empathetic, and caring.

And yet, she hadn't seemed one bit concerned about how Leesa would cope with losing her husband. Nor had she shown the slightest regret that Sven had died.

Was this a blind spot? My blind spot or hers? Did it say something about how the Nordstroms had treated Mert?

I couldn't imagine Leesa asking her cleaning lady to sit down and share a pizza. Sheila would never sit and eat with Linnea. My mother-in-law had this quaint belief that employees and employers should not fraternize. On the other hand, when Linnea's aunt had died last year, Sheila had been truly concerned for her maid's state of mind. Several times, Sheila had phoned Linnea to see how she was coping.

Had that been craven self-interest on Sheila's part? A totally phony interest, covering up Sheila's need to have Linnea back to work?

I didn't think so. I had walked in on Sheila while she and Linnea were talking. Sheila's back was to me, and she hadn't heard my approach, so the exchange must have been candid.

"Linnea, I am so sorry," she said. "I know your Aunt Tilly meant the world to you. It's a terrible loss. Yes, there will be a big hole in your life. That's the way of it. If I can do anything, let me know."

The sincerity in my mother-in-law's voice certainly seemed real enough.

Times like those convinced me I really did not know George's mother at all. The exchange seemed so contrary to all my experiences with Sheila. And yet...it was also strangely in character. Sheila could turn misty-eyed at the oddest moments. George had told me that her seemingly calloused exterior had been the result of years and years of getting her feelings hurt. That sounded rather unlikely to me.

If Sheila really didn't care about anybody but herself, how did I explain her love for Anya? Anya was too young to return the woman's affection in full. Whenever Anya soiled Sheila's clothes, and this happened frequently, my mother-in-law shrugged it off. That didn't seem like a self-centered person, did it?

Nor had she been cold-hearted when George's father, Harry,

died. We'd all known it was coming. Cancer had spread throughout Harry's body, into his bones and brain. While George had suggested his father be moved to a terminal care facility with hospice workers to attend him, Sheila had put her foot down.

"He will stay here at home, and I will be with him every minute of every day. That's the only way I can be sure he gets the proper care he needs."

By golly, she had proved as good as her word. During Harry's long goodbye, Sheila lost twenty pounds, weight she couldn't afford to drop. The family doctor threatened her with hospitalization and force-feeding.

"Over my dead body," she'd snapped.

Lying there in the bed in Anya's room, I began to drift away. My eyes grew more and more heavy; my thoughts fragmented. They scattered like dry leaves in an autumn rain storm. The last cogent thought I had was, "People are incredibly complex."

60

George was nowhere to be seen the next morning, but he did leave a note on the kitchen table: *Sorry I missed you both. Big deal in the works. Hope to get home at a reasonable hour tonight. Love to my girls — G.*

I wadded up the paper and tossed it into the recycling bin. While Anya ate her cereal, I dug around in my purse and found Advil. Downing the pills with a glass of water was the prelude to getting my mental house in order. After that, I went to work on brewing a fresh pot of coffee. Never had it seemed to take so long for the water to heat and percolate.

Before she'd left, Mert had told me she'd be able to get back the day after tomorrow. Or at least that was what I thought she'd said. Alcohol kills your brain cells, and if the pain in my skull was any indication, I had a cemetery rattling around between my ears. But the Advil started to kick in, and I could feel the ache get dimmer each minute.

I silently blessed the chemist who discovered ibuprofen.

After I poured myself a second cup of coffee, I was definitely feeling more human. Two lemon poppy seed muffins and a third cup later, I felt super-charged.

Taking in the mess around me, I did what any sensible woman would do after hiring on a cleaning lady. I threw myself into cleaning my house. I didn't want Mert to think I was a total pig. I couldn't take a chance on scaring her off.

Anya whimpered from her high chair. I decided to start picking up my house right after I changed Anya's diaper.

Once upstairs, the sight of the empty bed I'd slept in filled me with sadness, but I stiffened my backbone and put my baby on her changing table. "As soon as Mert gets this place cleaned up and the boxes are all broken down, you're going to get potty trained," I told my daughter as I peeled a soggy pair of Pampers off her sweet little Southern Hemisphere. The diaper pail was near to overflowing, and the pungent smell of urine wafted from the hamper in Anya's bathroom.

"All righty then. I'll dump the trash and then it's time to do laundry."

I hate to waste water, so I decided to grab a handful of George's dirty clothes, too. That would make a nice surprise for him, as he usually does his things himself, a habit he says he formed in high school.

"Well, old habits are made to be broken," I said. Anya was busy in her crib, playing with a toy that "talked." At the top of George's hamper sat the shirt he must have worn last night. I snatched it up.

Halfway to the washing machine, I stopped and sniffed the fabric. The strong scent of an expensive women's perfume wafted up at me. As I always do, I checked the garment for spots to treat. That's when I saw lipstick on the edge of his collar.

So he *was* cheating on me. Or was he?

Did I really want to know? Not really. Not right now.

I turned my thoughts elsewhere.

Had Sven Nordstrom been cheating on Leesa? Or she on him? Did it count as cheating, if having sex was your job? Did

Lars Larsen kill Sven because he needed Leesa for his movies? Or did Lars kill Sven, because he was in love with her?

Had Leesa killed Sven because he came between her and Lars? Was it remotely possible that Sven had been cheating on Leesa, and her ego couldn't take that, seeing as how she fancied herself a sex goddess?

Did Sven deserve to die? What would drive a woman to kill her husband? I slammed the lid on the washer, wishing George was in the tub. Impetuously, I flipped the water temperature to hot. Really hot.

An unfaithful spouse could drive anyone over the edge. Didn't the law see crimes of passion as less heinous than a premeditated murder?

Would poisoning your spouse count as a crime of passion? I didn't think so. Sven had been poisoned over a long period of time. How could an angry woman disguise her fury? Why didn't Sven realize that Leesa had something up her sleeve?

I stared at my washing machine. Red filled my field of vision. How dare he? Especially after he'd said he loved Anya and me! The urge to throttle George was strong. Stronger than I would have ever guessed.

But killing George wasn't my style. Not by a long-shot.

Anya's happy gurgle from the other room reminded me: My daughter needed her father.

George and I had made the best of a bad bargain, my unexpected pregnancy. He had never promised me more than he delivered, and I respected him for that.

After checking on my daughter, I ran back upstairs to the master bathroom and unloaded the hamper. In the full-length mirror, I caught a glimpse of an overweight woman with an unruly mop of curls. My reflection reminded me that I wasn't much of a prize.

If George was straying, maybe I deserved it. Maybe I needed to make more of an effort to entice him.

Maybe, if I saved him from a life behind bars, he would see our family was worth preserving. Because it was.

I knew that deep down, George Lowenstein was a good man. I'd seen him holding his father's hand, while Harry slipped from this world into the next. George had no illusions about Sheila. He'd told me bluntly, shortly after we'd decided to marry, "My mother is a force of nature. I love her, but I don't expect you to. Just know that she'd lay down her life for me. When she gets a notion in her head, she's unstoppable. She has incredibly high standards for herself and everyone she loves. Mom would throw herself in front of a Mac truck, if it saved me."

I didn't love Sheila. She didn't love me. But we were bound together for all time by our ferocious love of Anya. That also meant that saving George's butt was Priority Number One, no matter what he'd done or who he was seeing behind my back.

Hadn't I promised myself that I would not be run over, ignored, and put down?

Wasn't it up to me to make a change?

So my pants wouldn't zip. Big deal. I could buy a new pair. I could control my eating and quit shoving food down my throat, when I wasn't hungry, when my real goal wasn't feeding my body but had more to do with stuffing my feelings down.

Eating sugar was one of the many ways I tried, and failed, to cope with my sorrow. Now all those cookies had taken up residence and were building storage bunkers around my waistline.

I found another pair of maternity pants and pulled them on. With a long tunic top, I looked quite presentable.

I could start by tossing away that open package of Oreo cookies. With that stern directive in mind, I grabbed Anya and went downstairs into the kitchen.

"Anya, I have to get rid of all the sweets in our house."

She blinked at me with those incredible denim blue eyes. When I reached for the bag of Oreos in the cabinet, she looked at me quizzically. "Coo?"

"Cookie?"

"Coo?"

I got rid of the Oreos by eating the rest of the bag.

61

By blocking the threshold with boxes, I was able to let Anya crawl around on great room carpet. George had set up the TV first thing after we moved, so I put on *Dora the Explorer*. Anya stared at the globe-trotting cartoon character. Fueled by sugar from the Oreos, I buzzed around, opening boxes, tearing away packing paper, and sorting through contents.

Around noon, George phoned to see how we were doing.

I did my best to sound unaffected, but I could hear the stiff formality in my voice. I assured my husband that we were fine. He politely asked what I was doing. I told him, "Unboxing boxes."

"Um, it turns out that I'll be late tonight."

"No kidding. That's a surprise." The sarcasm in my words was sharp enough that Anya's head whipped around to stare at me.

"I thought we'd do something fun this weekend. Maybe go to a local park or go for a drive?"

"Right." I wasn't about to hop up and down with delirious

joy, because he thought he could see his way clear to spending time with us.

"I know it's been hard for you, what with me working such long hours and the house being in such disarray. I promise things are going to change." George hesitated, giving me an opening that I didn't take. He went on, "I talked with Robbie Holmes this morning. He had nothing but praise for you."

The compliment did take a little starch out of my britches. "Oh?"

"Yes, and he reminded me what a lucky guy I am. To have Anya...and you."

"Oh."

"He says there's been a breakthrough in the case. In fact, I got the impression that you might have pointed him in the right direction. Get this — Sven drank the poison over a period of weeks! It was probably in one of those sports drinks he was always chugging."

"Hmmm."

"Seems he kept a refrigerator full of them both at home and at his office. That's ironic, isn't it? Here he thought he was doing all this healthy stuff, but he was slowly poisoning himself. Taking those long rides in the morning must have made him drink more. In turn, that put more poison in his system."

I couldn't hold back any longer. "Robbie told me you knew Leesa apart from her being our neighbor. You never told me that."

"I didn't tell you that, because it's not true. Strictly speaking. My partner and I built the unit that houses the, uh, photography studio where she works. Remember? It's that strip mall over in Florissant? One of the first projects Bill and I ever completed."

"Yes. Sort of." I vaguely remembered the place he was referencing. It had been finished two weeks after Anya was born. I'd been so busy with motherhood that the whole job was a blur in my head.

"The guy who runs the studio kept calling us over and over, complaining that his power was out. I drove over to see if I could figure out what was happening. Turns out he'd plugged a bunch of power strips into one another. They aren't meant to be used that way, and they kept tripping the breakers."

"You knew her," I repeated. "Leesa. You never told me."

"She was there when I made the site visit. She had on a ton of makeup and a wig. I didn't recognize her, and frankly, I was too busy dealing with the problem at hand to pay her much attention. I told the guy in charge that we'd re-wire the unit. I figured it was a better option than letting the entire strip center burn to the ground. He was a total moron. I did my best to put the incident behind me."

"But you met Leesa and you never said anything!" I sounded petulant, because I was. George's round-about explanation had irked me. Why couldn't he just say, *Yes, I met her*?

"You aren't listening, Kiki! I didn't know who she was. She was all done up. I didn't pay attention to her because I was busy crawling around and looking at all the electrical sockets. I wasn't there to meet people. I was there to do my job. You have to understand. The day I showed up she was wearing a wig with short dark hair. Plus tons and tons of makeup."

"Were you introduced?"

"I don't remember. I was too busy trying to make sure the building didn't burn down. I have a feeling that ignoring her really honked her off. The first day after we moved in, she blocked me from backing out of the garage. When I rolled down the window, she asked why I hadn't asked for her autograph back at the studio. I still didn't recognize her. But then it clicked. I explained I wasn't into that sort of stuff, autographs and all. That really made her mad. She really flew off the handle. Man, does she have a temper. I told Robbie that I could see her killing Sven. He promised to look into it. Have you seen any activity over there? Paddy wagons pulling up and making arrests?"

"It's not like on TV. Mert told me as much."

"No, I imagine it's not. Let's keep our fingers crossed they solve this and there isn't a murderer in the neighborhood. Just think what that would do to our property value."

That made me laugh. Whatever else stood between us — or whoever else, as the case might be — George had the ability to crack me up.

After I said goodbye, I counted our shared chuckle as a point in the win column.

62

*A*round noon, I stopped unboxing long enough to feed Anya her lunch. She and I ate Vienna sausages with Kraft Macaroni and Cheese. Since a cloud cover threatened a rainstorm, a quick walk was in order, lest we miss a chance for appreciating the pretty red sugar maples on the next block. If the winds picked up, most of the vibrant leaves would be stripped from the branches.

We'd no more than gotten out the door when Anya screamed, "Doh!"

Coming out of the Nordstroms' open garage was dear Zoe, wagging her tail as she caught sight of Anya. Brita stuck her head out from around Sven's parked car. The older woman waved and beckoned for us to wait.

"Rain is in the forecast," she said, squatting down to tell Anya hello. Zoe had greeted my daughter with a lick to Anya's face that sent my baby into fits of giggles.

"Yes, I figured we'd better get our walk in now."

Brita fell into step with us. We admired the foliage all the way to the corner.

"Aren't you worried about leaving the garage door open?" I

hated to be so blunt, but I was concerned. "Is the house locked up? Have they caught the person who killed your brother?"

"No, they haven't. Unless it's happened and they haven't notified me. Zoe is a good watch dog. I doubt anyone will break in during broad daylight. Besides, that silly garage door seems to go up of its own accord."

"I've noticed that. I wonder what's happening. At first we thought that Sven and Leesa left it up on purpose. Then I asked, and that made your brother upset at me."

Brita's sad smile reminded me she was still grieving. Shoving her hands deeper into the pockets of her jeans, she nodded. "Yes, I thought they'd done it on purpose, too. I figured that Leesa was being careless. Maybe I've misjudged her on that, as well as on killing Sven. The police haven't found enough evidence to charge her. Not yet at least."

"Doesn't it scare you to be under the same roof as her?"

"No. She has no reason to hurt me. With Sven, there was a life insurance payout and her career to gain. I am nothing to her, other than a minor irritant. If she did hurt me, her actions would surely incriminate her. Besides, Zoe will protect me. Leesa's a little scared of her, and I've done nothing to ease her fears."

"Do the police have a suspect?"

"Not that I know of. I'm still waiting for Sven's body to be released. As I told you, Leesa insists that he be cremated. I want to take him to Minnesota and bury him in the family plot."

I couldn't think of an appropriate response so I simply said, "Of course."

"At first, I thought her insistence on cremation would make her more suspicious to the police. After all, if you poisoned someone, wouldn't you naturally want the body destroyed? But at this point, I doubt it matters. Assuming they've run all the tests they can on his...corpse."

A shiver seemed to overtake the woman, and she pulled her sweater around her more tightly. Either she was wearing the same jeans and sweater, or she had several nearly identical versions. In the harsh sunlight, Brita looked older and more tired than when we'd first met. With a start, I realized she must be nearly as old as Sheila. However, my mother-in-law would never let herself go like Brita had. Even after George's death, she had always appeared perfectly groomed and stylishly dressed.

The temperature was dropping, a prelude to the rain. Without conferring, we headed back the way we'd come.

"Look," I said. "George called to say he won't be home for dinner. Why don't you come over and eat with me? You can keep me company, while I unpack. Of course, Zoe is welcome, too."

We set a time and said goodbye. As I unlocked our front door, Brita and Zoe walked back into the Nordstroms' garage. Their arrival flushed out Bartholomew. The fluffy black cat shot out from under Sven's parked car, like a black bat out of a cave. Bart raced across the street and took cover in the overgrown lot.

"Bar?" Anya pointed at the disappearing feline. "Bye-bye?"

"Yes, honey. He's disappeared again, hasn't he?"

63

———

*T*he rest of the afternoon hurried by. Dinner would be easy. I'd planned a light version of "Hay and Straw" with a recipe I'd found in a magazine. The colorful pasta dish was close enough to macaroni and cheese to satisfy Anya, but adult enough to work for a guest.

I'd unboxed nearly all of the kitchen, which meant I could lay hands on the blender and pot. Having Brita's visit to look forward to lifted my spirits. Slowly, I was building friendships. First Maggie, then Mert, and now Brita. Of course, Sheila would have been quick to point out that Mert was a paid employee and that Brita would return home to Minnesota, but for a while, I could block out my mother-in-law's imagined put-downs. Instead, I let myself enjoy the fact that three new women had come into my life.

I'd hoped to make more friends in the neighborhood, but Leesa and I were never going to find common ground. That much was certain. That said, maybe Mrs. Bergen and I would get along. The next time I saw Mr. Bergen, I'd be more direct. I would suggest that he take me home and introduce me to his wife. After a face-to-face meeting, I could phone Alma Bergen and invite her over for coffee.

Yes, Maggie had been a practice run. Mert and Brita were successes. My new experiences were giving me much needed confidence. I planned to conquer the world, or at least part of it!

"Alma Bergen, prepare yourself. You're about to make a new friend," I said, staring out my kitchen window, as I rinsed off two dinner plates.

When the phone rang, I answered it absent-mindedly.

"You will not believe what just happened to me," George practically barked in my ear. "That stupid detective dropped by the office and wanted to talk. Here. In front of Bill and my staff."

"Robbie Holmes?"

"No. That twit who's been talking to you. Everwatt."

"Everbright."

"Ever-whatever. They've gotten the toxicology reports. They know what was used to poison Sven."

"What was it?"

"Something commonplace. He wouldn't tell me exactly, but he hinted around. Asked me if I did my own car maintenance. Is that a bunch of baloney or what?"

"Car maintenance?" Visions of flat tires danced in my head. What on earth would car maintenance have to do with Sven Nordstrom being poisoned?

"Right. I threw him out. I told him either he could arrest me or leave. He said he could come to the house with a search warrant. I have half a mind to call a lawyer."

"Maybe you should."

A shocked silence answered me. I added, "Mert was telling me that cops can twist a person's words around."

"Yeah, she's probably right. That's probably a good idea, about getting counsel. I'll talk to Mom. She'll know who I need to call. She's got a lot of contacts through the country club."

64

*B*efore hanging up, George reminded me that he wouldn't be home for supper. Once again, he brought up the idea of spending quality time together over the weekend. "Sure," I said, although my voice didn't hold much enthusiasm. "Whatever you want."

However, he was too distracted by his own problems to catch the flat intonation I'd used. Instead of biting on the bait I'd thrown out, he rattled on about visiting a park or even driving over to St. Albans, a darling nearby community.

"Right." I rinsed out two glasses. While the newsprint wrapping probably kept everything clean, I couldn't count on it. At last, I was having an adult dinner party. I hoped everything would be perfect for Brita's visit.

Promptly at five thirty, she rang the doorbell. Zoe sat patiently at her side. One ear was cocked with curiosity, but, otherwise the dog was as composed as any human guest might be.

Over one shoulder, Brita carried a bulging fabric bag. Over her other arm, she had a woven basket. To my surprise and delight, the woman gave me a hug.

It had been so long since someone had held me that I worried I'd burst into tears. Instead, I melted into the warmth. For a split second, I thought, "This is the reward I've needed. The mothering I've never had. I really do want more women friends in my life."

"Lo?" Anya sang out from her playpen. I led my visitors into the great room, where the fire glowed merrily without smoking. Zoe trotted over to Anya, who rewarded the Lab with a handful of Teddy Bear Grahams.

"All I need to do is throw the pasta into boiling water," I said. "The salads are prepared. The places are set. I didn't know what time you usually eat."

Brita smiled at me. "I brought dessert. A lingonberry torte. I'm happy to eat whenever it suits you, dear. This is very sweet of you. I know you have both hands full with unboxing and taking care of Anya."

We decided to open the bottle of chilled white wine that I'd selected to accompany our food. I put my feet up on a box and enjoyed the crisp flavor of apple with a hint of flowers I couldn't name. Brita pulled out her needlework.

"May I see it?"

She handed the hoop to me. I marveled at the tiny stitches. "What is this?"

"French knots. I'm using them on a drawstring jewelry bag. You make them by looping your thread around the tip of your needle. Let me show you."

She twisted her wrist, directing the silver tip of the needle in a clockwise direction three times. The size of the finished knot would be determined by the number of twists and by the size of the thread. "You try," she said as she handed the hoop to me.

My first knot appeared and promptly disappeared.

"You have to make sure the needle doesn't re-enter the same hole it came out of," Brita explained.

Slowly I got the hang of it. "Do you always use a hoop?"

"Yes, the tighter the fabric is the easier it is to work the knots." Taking the piece from me, she held it up to the light. "See those lighter areas? Where the light shines through? Those need more knots. They aren't packed densely enough."

I added more to the area I'd started. "This is sort of soothing."

"Yes, I find it to be. There's a rhythm to it, isn't there?"

We went online and looked at a variety of sites with patterns and examples of using French knots.

"Are you hungry yet?" I asked. When Brita said she was, I started a pot of water. She picked up Anya and brought her into the kitchen. From her command post in her high chair, my daughter threw Cheerios over the tray for Zoe to lick up off the floor.

"After we left you this afternoon, we saw Bart, the Bergens' black cat, come flying out of your garage." I stirred the pasta and checked that the sauce wasn't getting burned.

"Did you really?" Brita poured us both a glass of water. I liked how she made herself at home. "He's a beautiful animal, isn't he? Although one might argue that particular black cat really is bad luck."

"Why? Because he keeps running off? I bump into Mr. Bergen nearly every day, while he's out searching for Bart. I'll need to remember to tell him I saw the cat in the garage."

Brita inhaled sharply. "I would prefer that you don't. It will only upset the man."

"Why? He must be accustomed to Bart's wandering by now."

Brita sat rigidly in her chair. "Well, it's rather a long story and a sad one. You see, Anya isn't the only person who had a close encounter with Sven on his bike."

"No," I said. "I imagine not. The way Sven took curves and rode so fast, everyone would be fair game. Did he come close to hitting Bart? Is that why the cat races into the garage for shelter?"

She responded with a shake of the head.

I grabbed our salads out of the refrigerator and served first Brita and then me.

"More?" She offered me another glass of white wine. When I nodded, she poured me a glass and refilled hers as well. "I need a full glass or two for this story."

"Really?" I sipped mine, savoring the taste and the cool of the liquid, as it washed over my tongue.

"Yes. You see, just last year Sven rode his bike too close to Alma Bergen, while she was looking for Bart. He nearly clipped her."

Brita's voice trailed off. She had turned her attention to her salad. I offered her freshly ground pepper, which she refused. Once I could see she was ready to eat, I excused myself to finish our main course.

I stirred the cheese sauce one more time, drained the pasta, and tossed the ingredients together. After I served Brita, I served myself and put a smaller amount on a plate for Anya.

"Go ahead and eat while it's hot," I said. "I have to wait until Anya's is cool enough for her." Using a fork, I spread the pasta out, hoping it would cool faster.

"This is delicious." Brita smacked her lips appreciatively. "So is the salad. What are these white chunks?"

"Hearts of palm."

"I don't think I've ever had them before. What a nice texture and taste!"

I wanted to get back to what had happened with our neighbors. "You were saying that Sven rode too close to Alma?"

"Yes. Did you know that Talbot Bergen worked for Monsanto? Or maybe it was some other firm. Boeing? McDonnell Douglas? I can't recall. A brilliant man. In his day at least.

Not as much now. Growing old is hard. We all lose so much. Life piles up and wears you down."

"Mr. Bergen does seem to be a little lost. What exactly happened between his wife and Sven?"

"A bit of a mishap, actually. Alma didn't realize how close Sven was to her, until he was about a foot away. She jumped back — a startle reflex, really — and tripped over the curb."

"Gee, and I thought we had it bad because he'd put a scare into Anya. At least I didn't trip and he didn't hit the stroller."

"Right."

"I assume that's where she was, if Sven rode his bike too close to her. She couldn't have been on the sidewalk."

"You're correct. She was in the street and jumped backward. All because of that silly cat."

Brita's vehemence surprised me.

Anya picked up strands of pasta and put them in her mouth eagerly.

"It's that open garage door," I explained. "I've seen it go up by itself. I wonder if the safety sensor needs to be adjusted."

Brita cocked her head and stared at me. "I hadn't considered that. You might well be right. The last time I was down here it seemed fine."

"When was that?"

"A year ago. Sven invited me to come for Thanksgiving. He offered to pay for my gas so I could drive down. I would have noticed the door going up automatically. I don't remember seeing the cat in the garage, and I would have, because Zoe would have perked up with curiosity."

"I think Bartholomew follows field mice into Sven and Leesa's garage. George warned me that new construction such as ours can disturb their burrows. The tunnels offer them protect. After they're destroyed, the rodents seek shelter. Maybe Bart is trying to do you a favor by acting as a feline exterminator."

"Uh-huh." Brita chewed her food thoughtfully.

"I wonder if Alma even realizes how often her cat runs over to your brother's property? Since the Bergens face north and the Nordstrom house faces south, Alma might not know how often it happens." I picked up another mouthful of pasta.

Without looking up, Brita pulled her lips in tightly, like a purse drawn by its strings. For a minute, I worried she'd found a bug in her food or something equally unpleasant.

I lifted my glass and asked, "Did Alma hurt herself? Tripping over the curb?"

"Yes. Yes, as a matter of fact she fell down hard."

"Oh." I refilled our glasses. Brita pushed back her chair and rested her hands in her lap. She looked miserable.

"Sven swore to me that he wasn't really *that* close. He told me that he had control over his bike. But Alma spooked, like a horse does. Later we learned that Alma couldn't see or hear well. She was vain and refused to wear a hearing aid. I think she had blind spots in her field of vision. Sven and his bike appeared to her out of nowhere. Alma overreacted, lost her balance, and fell."

"Uh-huh." I'd heard this before.

"She landed hard on her side," Brita said, "and cracked her hip on the pavement."

"Sounds painful."

"Painful, yes. But..." Brita turned a wobbly smile at me. "How old are you?"

"Twenty-three."

"Just a child. A mere child."

I would have objected, but her tone was kind.

With a dry laugh, Brita shook her head. A trembling hand lifted a napkin to her eyes. Wiping them, she continued in a quivering voice, "Kiki, you're too young to realize this, but a broken hip in an elderly woman is a death sentence. Alma died two months after her fall."

─────────

65

I dropped my fork. "Alma Bergen is dead? You have to be kidding me."

"No, I'm not." Brita stared at me with such concern that I realized how unhinged I had sounded. "Why would that be so astonishing?"

"Because Talbot Bergen made it sound like Alma would invite me over! She's dead? You're telling me that his wife is gone?"

"Yes. I'm not surprised to hear he invited you over. I think he's losing his grip. Just yesterday I spoke to Talbot. We bumped into each other while I was walking Zoe. Talbot's still as feisty as ever, but he seemed confused." She smoothed the napkin in her lap. "Because you are young, you might not realize how much men depend on their wives. Not only do we live longer, but we also help them to live longer. We're caregivers. We monitor their health. We feed them properly. The list goes on and on. I imagine he has dementia."

This litany filtered through my experience, finally reaching the layer of my own marriage. Was I important to George? Did I give him a reason to get up in the morning?

Doubtful.

My soul-searching must have shown on my face.

"You haven't been married long," she said as she reached over and patted my hand. "As the years go on, you'll see what I mean. Our husbands may be rulers of the universe at work, but once they walk through that front door, they are little boys again. Dependent on us to make life easy, comfortable, and predictable."

"One might think that because Alma was older by five years, Talbot should have expected her to go first. But I happen to know that he married an older woman on purpose. You must remember, he was — is — a scientist. He'd done his research. He hoped to never face the twilight of his life alone. Besides, Alma never acted like the older of the two. She was vibrant. Lively. Engaged. Alma was Talbot's lifeline to the world at large. She would invite people over to eat. She was a one-woman Welcome Wagon, extending a helping hand, bringing over treats, and asking how she could help. Yes, Alma was Talbot's link to the world outside his lab."

"Was Leesa that for Sven?" I was turning over pieces and trying to see how they fit.

"No. But Sven was that for Leesa. In their marriage, the roles were reversed. He was the adult, and she was the child. I believe he kept her from growing up. Even now, she's lost without him. She's been adamant that Sven's cremation be done immediately. When I asked why, she said she couldn't stand to think about the decay. That's all that mattered to her! How he would look!"

"Wow."

"Yes, she's really something, isn't she? I explained I'd take care of it all. Finally, she agreed, as long as she didn't have to look at his remains. I had no idea how expensive it would be to ship his body back to Minnesota. The transport alone will cost me $2000. The money will have to come out of savings."

"Can you afford that?"

"I'm on a fixed income. To cover an expense this large, I'll have to make economies, but I'm bound and determined to manage. May I make myself at home and start coffee? I'd like a cup of decaf with my dessert. How about you?"

66

———————

Brita stayed about an hour longer. We discussed cooking, doing hand embroidery, and her long trip back to Minnesota. Zoe's presence delighted Anya, especially when she managed to say, "Zo-oh," and call the black Lab over. Brita and I applauded my daughter's precocious efforts at animal handling.

By the time I locked the front door behind my guest, I was tuckered out. Anya could barely keep her eyes open, too. Although I rarely think about it, I'm an introvert. I need alone time to recharge my batteries. I've read up on the differences in personality types, and extroverts scoop up energy interacting with other people, whereas I get depleted. Maybe that was one reason it had been hard for me to make new friends. Each person drained my batteries, even as I craved the support of friendship.

Brita had left behind the lingonberry torte. Only a mighty effort on my part kept me from finishing it off, but I did manage a modicum of self-control. I wrapped the leftovers carefully and put them in the refrigerator before carrying Anya upstairs to bed.

"Doh? Zo-oh?" She pointed to the foyer. "Bye-bye?"

"That's right, honey. The dog's name is Zoe, and she's gone bye-bye. You liked seeing her, didn't you? I promise that one day we'll have a dog. Or a cat. Or both. You would like that, wouldn't you, sweet pea?"

After bathing her and putting her in the crib, I fell asleep on the twin bed in Anya's room, but not before reviewing every word of my conversation with Brita. Tomorrow, I planned to Google how breaking a hip could kill an older adult woman. It didn't make sense to me, but Brita had sounded sure of herself.

I also wanted to Google Talbot Bergen and find out more about his background. My mind flitted back to what Brita had said as she'd hugged me goodbye.

"You are a lucky woman, Kiki. You might not realize it, but you are."

"Why do you say I'm lucky?"

She stroked Anya's curls. "Having a child is one of life's greatest joys. You've already discovered that your heart lives outside of your body. No one understands his or her parents until becoming a parent. But even more than that, having a child is a life-affirming event. It's a badge of womanhood. For those who've tried and failed, it's the ultimate deep wound, a repudiation of all other accomplishments."

I'd grown accustomed to the long words that Brita used as a natural part of speech. Big words were her currency. But after two glasses of wine and a busy day, I couldn't follow her drift.

"I'm not sure I understand," I said. "Could you explain yourself?"

"Leesa can't have children. Ever. It's a biological impossibility. I don't know the particulars, just the end result. She's channeled her frustration into an alternate form of perfection. It's like an apple that's perfect on the outside and rotten at the core. Only, she's constantly polishing that exterior, trying to prove that she's okay. When you moved in, seeing your adorable daughter must have been a crushing blow to her ego."

Lying on my back, I ran my hands over my jelly-belly. Because I'm short, Anya had stretched my muscles and skin to the max. I doubted my gut would ever go back to normal. Not that I'd ever been flat-bellied, but I'd never worn a spare tire around my waist, like now.

Maybe instead of hating that roll of flesh, I should bless it. I should remember that it had sheltered, nurtured, and fed my daughter for nine months. I should recall that this part of my body had served as an incubator for the most adorable chick ever.

Was Leesa more desirable, just because she was thin?

Our culture put such a premium on being slender.

But she hadn't given birth, so her body had never been put to the test or pushed to the limits of its endurance. What had my ob/gyn said about the rigors of labor? "It's like driving a Ferrari into a concrete wall at 100 miles per hour. Giving birth is that rough on a woman's organs."

Yet, I'd come through that car wreck with a beautiful, healthy child. Every step of the way, my body had known what to do without help from my conscious mind. Wasn't that praise-worthy? Unlike the missteps while learning to walk or talk, my body had mastered pregnancy without any practice. Pretty nifty stuff, when you thought about it.

Leesa's perfect body had failed her, while mine had done me proud.

Why did I even bother to compare myself to Leesa?

Maybe because we lived in a culture where women were encouraged to compare themselves to each other? Where women's looks were assigned numbers, like, *She's a ten*? Or where women competed with each other publicly and were awarded prizes on the basis of their looks? Where public figures remarked on how attractive or unattractive women were — but kept mum about the looks of men? Where the ages, and sometimes the weights, of women were a common part of their biographies?

What a cruel way to judge another human being — and, yet, didn't I do the same? Could I enter a room and not size up my "competition"? Could I mingle with other women and not find myself evaluating how attractive they were?

How did I benefit from such silly behavior?

I didn't. I only hurt myself by thinking these thoughts.

And yet, I knew better. But I'd still done it! I railed against such sexism, even though I secretly participated by judging myself and other women, holding us up to an impossible standard.

How much rougher would I be on myself, if I couldn't have a child and wanted one? Wouldn't I feel let down? Angry? Confused? How would I channel all the energy, the tsunami of guilt, disappointment, and anger?

Might I not focus on the aspects of my body I *could* control, like my looks? Wasn't that what Leesa had done? Wouldn't it become my obsession?

But honestly, I, too, was obsessed with my looks in a twisted sort of way. My focus was putting myself down and beating myself up.

Maybe Leesa and I were two sides of a coin.

Both doing our best to get through life and feel good about ourselves.

67

The next morning when I woke up, George was making coffee in the kitchen. Anya was still asleep, leaving my husband and me with a little one-on-one time. As usual, he was freshly groomed, looking sharp with his white Oxford cloth shirt, striped tie, and navy wool suit. I always admired that about him. To George, dressing down was a nice pair of khaki pants and a polo shirt. He started each day with a shower and a shave. He always smelled terrific, thanks to the expensive cologne he wore.

I told him about Brita's visit.

"Sounds like you had a good time." There were dark circles under his eyes. I had a hunch he'd gotten home late. The raccoon-ish look confirmed it.

"I did. How was your evening?"

"Not pleasant." He stirred his coffee with care. "I had to tell someone that we wouldn't be interested in working with them in the future. That we wanted to end our association. It was difficult, but necessary."

I noticed that he'd mixed his pronouns, first saying "someone" and then "them." It wasn't like George to be imprecise with his grammar. He was holding back a part of his message, but the late night and wine had left me muzzy headed. I wasn't sure how to decipher what he really meant.

Rather than ask, I mumbled, "Bummer. That sounds like it wasn't much fun."

George reached over to intertwine his fingers with mine. "Kiki, I've been thinking a lot about us. I want to be a better husband and father. I'm going to try to spend more time with you and Anya. You're important to me. I mean, both of you are. The other night, when I was here alone with Anya, I realized you're here with her all the time. It was, frankly, scary. Having that much responsibility."

"You're right. I worry every minute that she'll hurt herself. Get into something that's dangerous, while I'm not paying enough attention. She's cruising these days. Holding onto the furniture and walking like a champ. Before, she'd take a few steps and land on her butt. Now, she's all over the place when she's not in her playpen or the crib. I even feel guilty that I keep her penned up as much as I do."

"I can see you've made progress, getting the boxes moved around and unpacked. I guess there isn't much you can do, cleaning-wise, until they're out of the way."

"Yes. Some of them are your things. I have no idea what to do with your stuff."

"I think Mom was happy to unload as much as she could on us. I looked in one of the boxes this morning and saw toys I played with as a boy! Who knew she'd be so sentimental?"

"Speaking of your mom, have you heard more from Robbie Holmes?" I stood up and poured myself a bowl of Grape Nuts, before refilling George's coffee cup and mine.

"Not directly. He told Mom they're closer to making an arrest. I did call an attorney, an old family friend from temple, Richard Heckman. He got back to me late last night and said I was off the hook. Your explanation of how my fingerprints got on Sven's bicycle was a turning point."

That explained why he was all lovey-dovey this morning.

But did it matter? Maybe he had needed a reminder that we were in this together. If it had come as a result of defending him, so much the better.

A strobing red light flashed against the wall of our foyer. With cereal bowl in hand, I turned and walked toward the formal dining room.

"Kiki?" George called after me.

"George? You have to come and see this."

"What on earth?" He took his place beside me.

Two policemen marched a handcuffed Brita Morgenstern down the sidewalk. Putting one hand on her head, a uniformed cop helped her into the back seat of the squad car.

fter George left for work, I turned on the news. Every local channel carried the story of Brita Morgenstern's arrest. Unfortunately, none of them offered clues as to why she was the suspect.

I paced the floor, feeling more and more desperate to know her situation. If she was the killer, should I be worried about her having spent so much time in our house?

Mert phoned around noon. "I had a cancellation. Thought I'd swing by and work at your place this afternoon, if that'll suit you."

Of course it would. I phoned Sheila and asked if she could pick up Anya. "If you can help out, I can totally devote myself to getting this place picked up. I worry about Anya getting into something and getting hurt."

"That's good thinking on your part. I'll be there in fifteen minutes."

My mother-in-law pulled in right as the cleaning lady parked her truck. Anya squealed with delight at the sight of two of her favorite people.

"George phoned me to say you'd watched them load that

murderer in the police car." Sheila used her chin to point at the Nordstroms' house.

"I don't think Brita did it." I reached down to pick up Anya's diaper bag and hand it over.

"Of course she did." Sheila sniffed with irritation, while she slid the diaper bag over one shoulder. Because it was blue and green, the satchel went well with the navy slacks and sweater she was wearing, picking up the colors in the silk scarf at her neck.

"Brita was up in Minnesota, until after Sven died. How could she have done it?" I spoke passionately. I hated the idea that I'd been entertaining a killer. More importantly, I was not about to dump the rest of the lingonberry torte. No way. And, if Sheila knew that Brita had left food for us, she would have stood over me while I tossed out the dessert. I knew she would. She was food-resistant, while I clung to it like Velcro.

"She must have put something in his food or his shampoo to kill him over time," Mert said, leaning against a doorframe. "That's why poisoners are so hard to catch. They can do it, walk away, and wait."

"But you two don't know Brita, and I do." I bit my lip rather than explain that she'd been here last night, eating with me. That might send both Sheila and Mert into a tizzy.

"You only *think* you know her," Sheila said. "Waving to a person across the street isn't exactly what I'd call a relationship."

"Okay, maybe we aren't bosom buddies, but we have spoken to each other frequently."

The three of us adults had inched our way into my house. Even in the dim light, Sheila's worry lines were pronounced. Mert also had a concerned expression on her face. Their glances at each other confirmed they were worried about me.

"Look, Brita has a beautiful black Lab named Zoe. Anya's

crazy about animals." I shrugged. "It was natural I'd get to know the woman."

"Sounds like that dog is about ready to become homeless." Mert crossed her arms over her chest.

"It's not Brita. She is very, very nice. Sven was her baby brother. What motive would she have had for killing him?"

"Life insurance." Sheila lifted her chin and looked down at me. "He'd taken out two policies. One paying his wife and the other paying his sister. Those women will be rolling in the dough. That's what Robbie told me."

Her quick answer felt like a punch to the gut. All the air whooshed out of my mouth. "Ahhhhh."

"Let's go, Anya," Sheila said, picking up my daughter. "Would you like to spend the night with me? Hmm, darling?"

How like Sheila not to ask me first. I briefly considered dressing her down, but what was the point? All I'd accomplish would be a waste of energy.

I kissed my daughter goodbye. "Thank you for doing this, Sheila."

She scowled. "George deserves a nice, clean house."

"Right." Because I was annoyed at her about Brita, I added, "So do I."

69

"That there mother-in-law of yours is a piece of work," Mert said, when we took our first break.

She had hauled in a cart full of cleaning supplies and gone at the place with a speed that rivaled a tornado. Starting at the ceiling fans, she'd dusted each room from top to bottom, finishing by vacuuming up what she'd disturbed.

She'd also brought along a portable air filter. "I got to thinking about how much of this here dust we'd be spreading. We want to trap it, and this'll do just that."

Most of the containers were half-filled and stuffed to the brim with paper. The movers had charged us by the box. Using a lot of these made sense from their standpoint. It also insured less breakage. Once the boxes were broken down, there really wasn't that much to put away. I'd opened a box in the great room and quickly pulled out piles of books. The open shelves on either side of the fireplace would make a lovely spot for them.

Mert and I sat down to re-heated pasta. We both dug in. She wielded her fork like a lethal weapon, attacking the food. Although I felt slightly guilty about it, I didn't offer to share the lingonberry torte. Instead, I kept it tucked away in my refrigerator, my personal stash of happiness.

Of course, my conscience wouldn't go stand in a corner and shut up like a good girl. Over and over, my thoughts returned to the dessert. From there it was a short hop to Brita and our conversation.

"You're awful quiet." Mert stared at me.

"Yup."

"You okay? Worried about your neighbor?"

"Yes."

"Wanna turn on the news? We can watch it from in here, right?"

"Right." I found the remote control and pushed one of the few buttons I knew how to use, the On/Off switch. Next, I tampered with my other fave, the Volume control. Sure enough, we quickly learned that Brita was in custody. She would stay there, because she'd told the court that she couldn't post bond.

"That's it!" I jumped out of my seat.

"What?" Mert regarded me through narrowed eyes.

Without answering her, I grabbed my cell phone and called Robbie Holmes. Mert listened while I explained to him about Brita's visit the night before.

"She told me that she would have to cut back her expenses and take money out of savings to ship Sven's body back to Minnesota. According to the news report, she couldn't make bail. Doesn't that prove she isn't expecting a windfall? Wouldn't she have been less concerned about spending her savings, if she was sure she was Sven's beneficiary? Think about it, Robbie. It doesn't make sense. Anyone who felt financially secure wouldn't think twice about borrowing from savings to post bail. Who'd want to spend a night in jail? I sure wouldn't! I'd pay to get out, wouldn't you?"

Robbie didn't interrupt. When I paused to take a breath, he

said, "That's an interesting point. As I told you, this isn't m jurisdiction. For all I know, Everbright has a lot of solid evidence."

"What if he doesn't? What if he's looking in the wrong direction? A friend told me that once cops get a theory, they don't give up easily." I shot a quick look at Mert. She nodded her agreement.

"That's because we're usually right. If the creep didn't do what he's accused of, you can bet he's pulled another stunt and should get locked away."

"But you'll talk to Everbright? Share with him what Brita told me? Robbie, you have to realize this was after two and a half glasses of wine. She had no reason to lie to me. None."

"Okay, you've got my attention."

"Then let me add one other point. You said that the person who killed Sven had ongoing access to him. Brita hasn't been here for months. She was last down here a year ago at Thanksgiving time. Sven paid for her gas."

"Maybe she was too smart to keep coming down and visiting," Robbie said. "Maybe she didn't want to leave a trail. Poisoners are not generally impulsive. They are planners. Maybe she tainted something and left it behind for Sven to ingest."

"That's pretty random, don't you think?"

"I'm not sure that the evidence backs you up. We deal in cold, hard facts. That's what we have to present to a judge or jury. However, I do see your point."

I hung up feeling slightly better. I'd gotten Robbie to question whether Brita was guilty.

"Ready?" Mert raised an eyebrow at me. "If you're done playing Nancy Drew, let's get back to the task at hand."

70

By four o'clock, I'd had enough. All my muscles hurt. My hands were rough and cracked from smoothing out sheets of newsprint. A damp film of perspiration covered my torso. We'd worked steadily without a break.

Mert was wiping her forehead on her sleeve, a sign that she too was tired.

"Got anything else we can eat? I need a snack," she said. "Something to tide me over?"

When I opened the refrigerator door, she peered inside. The lingonberry torte sat front and center. Even half-eaten it was gorgeous. My mouth began to water at the magenta berries coupled with the scent of almonds.

"Is that what I think it is? A lingonberry torte? Where on this green earth did you dig one of them up? I ain't had that in ages."

"Really?" I rummaged through the drawers and pulled out a soggy bag of baby carrots, a stiff slice of American cheese, and a package of turkey lunch meat well past its expiration date. There was no help for it; I'd have to share.

Mert couldn't take her eyes off the treat.

"Years ago, I lived next to a bakery run by a bunch of Swedes.

They used to make lingonberry tortes once't a week. Man, oh, man, I loved them. Where'd you buy that?"

Getting two plates out of the cabinet, I cut and deposited two slices. "Um, warm?"

"Just enough to take the chill off."

I kept my back to her while I popped hers in the microwave. With any luck, she would quit worrying about where the pastry came from. I knew in my heart that Brita wasn't guilty, and I had no fear of eating the dessert. After serving the warmed slice to Mert, I heated mine slightly, too.

"Man, oh, man. This is good. Who baked it?" She was licking her fork.

"Uh..." Sinking into my chair, I closed my eyes and savored the sweet tang.

"Kiki?"

The inflection warned me. Mert was onto my secret. She repeated, "Kiki? I asked you a question." This time her voice was more insistent.

"Yeah?" I had been magically transported to another planet. I was not about to let Mert spoil this for me.

"Did Brita make this?"

"Um...she brought it over last night."

"You have to be kidding me! Your neighbor is a poisoner, and you're eating her food? Are you TSTL?"

"What on earth is TSTL?"

"Too Stupid To Live!"

"No, but I do have a sweet tooth, and I'm hungry."

Crash! Mert slammed her fist against the tabletop, causing the plates and forks to shiver as if a train had run past. "Are you nuts?"

"Brita didn't do it, Mert," I said. "I know she didn't. I ate part of this dessert last night, and I feel just fine. I trust her. And, if you don't trust her, slide your plate over here. I don't want this torte to go to waste."

"Have you lost your mind?"

"I think we've established that my grip on reality is precarious."

"And you fed this to me?"

"I didn't want to. I wasn't planning to share." I reached for her plate.

She slapped my hand and nibbled a tiny piece of torte. "I'm thinking; I'm thinking."

"Better kick it into overdrive, or I'm going to grab your dessert and make up your mind for you."

She growled at me.

"Look. I am not crazy. Trust me. Brita is not guilty."

71

The ringing of my phone interrupted my impassioned defense of Brita and the lingonberry torte. I hunched over my plate to keep Mert away while I answered the call.

"Kiki? I need a favor." Brita sounded breathless.

For one scary heartbeat, I thought that maybe she'd made a prison break. What would I do if she asked me to drive her over state lines? Loan her money or my car? Instead, she barreled ahead with a perfectly reasonable request. "Zoe is all alone. She's old. I don't think Leesa will want take care of her properly. I'm worried about my dog."

"Sure, sure, no problem. Brita, are you okay? Have they treated you fairly? I'll see to Zoe, but do you need a lawyer?"

"I have called my minister up in Minnesota. He is seeing what he can do. But my poor Zoe. She is —" and Brita's voice cracked before she whispered, "alone."

"Of course I'll take care of her. Nothing would give me more pleasure." Realizing how that might be taken, I amended what I said with, "Under the circumstances, I mean."

"I am very relieved. You have taken an enormous load off my shoulders."

"Brita? I know you didn't do it. They'll have to let you out." A feeling of helplessness washed over me.

"I hope so. This isn't a very good spot to be in. Not at all." A sob broke through the distance between us.

"Do you want me to find a lawyer?"

"No. I trust my minister. He'll know what to do. He is making calls. If you could help with Zoe that would take a load off my mind."

"Of course."

An authoritative voice in the distance told her that she needed to cut our call short.

"Brita, don't worry about Zoe. Anya and I will take good care of her. I promise." Reluctantly, I said goodbye.

Mert had been watching me curiously, while eating every bit of her torte. I explained what I'd heard. "I bet that poor dog hasn't been out all day."

"Then you got yourself a perfect reason to walk across the street and play Sister Snoop." Mert chuckled.

"I'm not a snoop." Blood rushed to my face. "If you'll recall, I've been dragged into this. Three cop visits in less than a week."

"Whatever." Mert grinned at me. "I love reading about amateur sleuths."

"What can an amateur do that a professional can't?" I grabbed my house keys and shoved the last bite from my plate into my mouth.

"They can see how people interact. Watch folks in their natural habitats. Ain't you ever read anything by Agatha Christie?"

"Yes. You coming?" I aimed to cut the conversation short and do what I could for Zoe. "Let's go."

We trooped out my front door with all the determination of two women on a mission. I didn't worry about Leesa being nasty to me, because I had Mert by my side. Mert struck me as the sort of person who could handle whatever Leesa threw our way.

"What?" Leesa opened the door and scowled at me. At her feet was the blue bin. Evidently we'd interrupted her on her way to put out the recycling. "Why is cleaning lady with you?"

"Um, Brita phoned and asked me to take care of Zoe."

Leesa's chilly demeanor thawed a little. "I do not know dogs. You will take? Right now? Good, but wait. I must put out garbage."

This young woman had no social graces at all. Or, if she did, she didn't bother to waste them on us. Instead of stopping to get Zoe, Leesa walked past us and set the tub beside the curb.

"Is done," she said, brushing off her hands.

"Like I was saying, I'd be happy to take care of the dog for as long as necessary. I love animals, and Anya is absolutely crazy about Zoe." Staring at the perfectly made-up face and trim physique, I reminded myself of what I'd learned the night before.

Leesa was all alone. Sort of. I had no idea how close she was to any of her girlfriends or to the people who'd shown up at her party. Maybe Lars would come over and comfort her. Who knew?

But she didn't have a child and I did. Her husband was dead. I couldn't imagine the sort of emptiness she must feel.

While Mert and I waited on the portico, Leesa shut the door in our faces. I stood there, nose nearly touching the crackled green paint. It felt like I'd been slapped. The tightness of anger clogged my throat. I would have turned and walked away, but Mert grabbed my arm.

"Just roll with it. She's different." Mert lifted and dropped a shoulder.

And, of course, Zoe was on the other side of the barrier.

The door opened, and Leesa passed me the leash. Zoe happily trotted to my side.

"Food and dishes," Leesa said, handing a heavy mesh bag to Mert. "Dog needs to peepee. Your problem now."

"Yes. Thanks."

As we stepped off the stoop, I whispered to Mert, "Anya will be thrilled."

"Yeah, that little girl of yours'll be in hog heaven, for sure. Don't think your hubby is gonna be happy. But that's another thing entirely."

"How's the bag?" I asked. "Are you okay with it?"

She assured me that the weight of the dog food and dishes didn't bother her at all. As we ambled past the open garage door, a black shadow came flying out. Zoe cocked an ear but didn't seem bothered. Her tail wagged as she walked obediently by my side.

"There goes Bart. The king of the open garage door." I explained to Mert what I'd learned about Alma chasing the cat and ultimately taking a fall that killed her. "I can't believe it. A simple fall and then she dies?"

"Breaking a hip causes all sorts of complications. Less mobility and a bigger chance of ending up in a nursing home to name just two. Shoot-fire, I ain't even sure they've explored all the reasons it's such a problem. But it is practically a death sentence."

Those last words hit me hard. Was Brita also looking at a death sentence? Could the police prove she'd killed her own brother? I gave myself a little shake, trying to get rid of my gloomy thoughts.

After we crossed the street, Zoe squatted in the overgrown lot. When she had finished, she pulled toward my house.

"I wonder if I should make her stay outside a little longer. See if her tank is really empty," I said.

"Why bother?" Mert asked. "In dog years, she's got a lot more experience than you do. If she has to go, she'll let you know."

72

*B*rita had put a lot of trust into her pastor. Too much trust for my taste, but I didn't know him and she did. Other than fret and light a candle, I could not do more for my new friend than to take good care of her beloved pet.

Zoe nudged me with a cold nose. Her brown eyes searched my face, as though she was waiting for me to confirm that everything would be all right. I told her as much and gave her a hug. She smelled of dog and cedar from her bed.

Leesa insistence that she take out her recycling rather than transfer the dog reminded me I needed to sort our waste materials as well. Thanks to Mert's help, we'd knocked down a lot of boxes. The pile of blank newsprint was growing at a satisfying rate.

Zoe sat by my side while I sorted the trash in the garage. The hum of the vacuum signaled that Mert was doing a final pass before gathering her cleaning equipment and supplies. Still, sorting the recyclables made me feel virtuous. It was also something that George and I were both passionate about. Sheila thought we were nuts. She didn't believe in recycling.

"How can you not believe?" I'd asked. "This isn't a fantasy like the tooth fairy. It's science."

"It's baloney. You do all that dirty work and they dump everything into one big pile. It all goes to the same landfill."

I didn't care. If it even helped just a little, it was a step in the right direction. While stacking up the boxes, I put the newsprint aside. After flattening it out and folding it, I realized it would make the perfect raw material for papier mâché. Suddenly, the desire to get back to crafting hit me hard. How had I lost the urge? The answer: I'd buried it in the hustle-bustle of daily life. With a sigh, I sorted the heavy solid items. Once they were in the bin, it looked nearly empty.

While Mert loaded her things in the truck, I lugged the recycling tub to the curb, cringing as rivulets of water dripped down my pants legs. Inside were tin cans, two Diet Dr Pepper cans, a dozen baby food jars, a plastic container from cottage cheese, and a stack of flattened cereal boxes.

"Let's go inside and look at a calendar and figure out when we can finish this here job up." Mert slammed her door shut.

Zoe never left my side. She was such a good dog.

"Right. How much more do we have to do? What's your estimate?"

"At least a whole day. Probably more like one and a half. Depends on if you want me to tackle the garage and outside? Them there windows of yours are covered with dirt. It's a wonder you can see out."

I didn't have a calendar on me, because I hadn't needed one, but she did. We walked back inside. There I found a scrap of paper to take notes on. I also wrote Mert a check.

"Believe me, you're worth your weight in gold, but this will have to do."

After cracking open two celebratory cans of Diet Dr Pepper, We settled on a time two days away. "Of course, iff'n I get a break or a cancellation, I'll come straight here. Or would you rather I phone you first?"

"You're always welcome here," I said, and I meant it.

"That's nice to hear." Mert gave me a hug.

I'd gone back to breaking down boxes when Mert phoned.

"When I was pulling away, I noticed your recycling bin. You ought to rinse out them there windshield washer fluid bottles. That stuff tastes sweet. If the dog or that black cat licks up the fluid, they could die."

"What windshield washer fluid bottles are you talking about?"

"The ones in your recycling. You must have a dozen or more."

"Are you sure you were looking at the right bin? I just took my recycling out, remember? When I sorted it, there weren't any bottles in there. Certainly there weren't any bottles of windshield washer fluid."

"Yours is right by your driveway. It couldn't belong to no one else."

I looked out the window. "Yeah, it is sitting there by its lonesome, but I promise you I did not put any windshield fluid bottles in it."

"Then you got pixies in your neighborhood, and they like clean car windows, 'cause you sure got a passel of bottles in that blue bin."

With that, she said goodbye.

I left Zoe inside, while I went out to see if Mert was right. Of course, she was.

Curious about Mert's claim that the liquid could sicken Zoe or Bart, I read the label.

And all the hairs stood up on the back of my head.

73

I circled the blue bin, staring at the pile of empty containers. "I have to calm down," I said out loud.

Where had the bottles had come from? No one was near for me to talk to, so I kept up a steady conversation with myself.

"This can't have anything to do with Sven's death. It can't be the poison they're looking for. Why would he drink windshield fluid? That's crazy. These didn't come from our house. That's not possible. I know what I put in that bin, when I sorted things. But where did they come from?"

Pulling my phone from my pocket, I stood there in the street and called George at work. I didn't bother with a greeting. Instead, I plunged right in. "Did you dump a bunch of windshield fluid bottles in our recycling bin?"

"No. Of course not. I've been at work all day."

"So you never emptied or owned any bottles of windshield fluid?"

"No. I go to that full-serve station over on Conway once a month. They top off all my fluids. Remember? I told you that you should do that, too."

"You are absolutely, one hundred percent positive that you

haven't purchased any windshield fluid bottles or used any windshield fluid in our cars? You didn't box any up to bring to our new house?"

"Absolutely not. Why would I? The full-serve station always checks my oil levels and my other fluids." He paused. "Why? Do you need windshield fluid?"

"I'm fine. Just asking." With that, I ended the call. Walking back into the house, I emptied a smallish box. Taking it to the curb, I studied the empty bottles of windshield fluid. Rather than touch them directly, I took the bottom hem of my tee shirt and used it like an oven mitt to cover my skin. Holding a bottle up to the light, I could see that the fluid was icy blue.

I'd seen that color of liquid before. I reached for the memory, but it eluded me. It danced just beyond my grasp, taunting me.

Where had I seen it?

Was it really the same as I remembered?

Was I putting two and two together and coming up with six?

I glanced over at the Nordstroms' garage. As usual, their door was up. Was Bart wandering inside? Had Leesa tossed any bottles that might do the cat harm?

I jogged across the street and looked in her bin. Nothing was there but fashion magazines, a cereal box, and an old newspaper.

Back on my side of the street, I grabbed the lightweight box and carried it back inside my garage. Tucking one set of flaps under the other, I closed it up. For good measure, I ran inside the house and grabbed packing tape. As I sealed the box, I thought over what I knew, what I'd seen, and what I suspected. I put the sealed box back in the recycling bin. No way could an animal get to it now.

I called Robbie Holmes. He didn't answer, but I got his answering machine. I asked him to get back to me. Almost as an afterthought, I said, "By the way, I just found a bunch of windshield washer fluid bottles in my recycling bin. Neither George nor I bought them. Isn't that weird?"

As I ended the call, a thought occurred to me. What if another neighbor, someone farther down the street, had dumped extra bottles into our bin? If so, Bart could get into those.

"Kitty, kitty?" I called. I didn't get a response. It was entirely possible that Bart was inside his home and safe. But, then again, he was such a little sneak. Who knew where he was?

Hitting the garage door button, I jumped over the beam of the electric eye and headed toward the Bergens' house.

74

*E*nid opened Talbot Bergen's front door. Today she wore a good amount of makeup, tight jeans, and a low-cut blue top with faux gems around the neckline. The change in her appearance shocked me. She'd gone from mousy to provocative. What was that all about?

"I hope you aren't trying to sell something." Her voice sounded defiant.

"No, I just wanted to speak to Mr. Bergen."

"He is resting." Her eyes flicked to a hallway. "Lately, he's been taking little naps. Especially after his walk."

"I dropped by to warn him not to let Bart wander around."

"Has that old cat been bothering you?"

"I'm worried about him getting into trouble."

"What a Romeo." She shook her head. "You'd never guess he's been neutered. No matter how hard we try to keep him inside, he slips past us faster than we can close a door."

"It's not about his love life. I'm worried about him getting sick."

"Sick?" She raised an eyebrow. After glancing at her watch,

she seemed to relax. "Why would he get sick? Look, I've got a little time. Would you like a cup of coffee? Tea?"

"Sure. Tea, please." I followed her into a spotless kitchen. Modern white cabinets and a granite countertop suggested it was new, but the appliances particularly intrigued me. They were top-of-the-line machines with the most cutting edge electronic gadgetry available. Standing there, I gawked at the blinking lights.

"Talbot loves his toys," Enid said. She moved elegantly from the coffee pot to the cabinet and then to the refrigerator, collecting items to serve our drinks. "As for the appliances, he loves anything new. Wants to know how everything works. He is always reading and thinking. He's very curious."

Rather than wander around, and I wanted to, I pulled out a chair and sat down. "You must enjoy Mr. Bergen's company."

"I love Talbot to pieces."

It took all my willpower not to react. This seemed completely inappropriate. It was also none of my business.

"Yes," she continued. "I just adore him. He's been like a second father to my boy, Marshal. Marshal thinks he's wonderful, and Talbot loves spending time with him. Talbot never had a boy of his own. He and Alma only had the two girls. Of course they aren't girls now. They are grown women."

"I don't think I've seen them around." I wanted to keep her stream of commentary going.

"Don't get me started." Her mouth screwed up into a twisted pout. "Those two are absolutely spoiled rotten. Never worked a day in their lives. Snotty as all get out. And selfish? It's a crime. They can't be bothered to make time for him. They're disgusting."

"So the daughters hired you? Because of his Alzheimer's?"

"What? Who said he has Alzheimer's? That's not true! Talbot

is sharp as a tack. Sometimes he doesn't sleep well. Occasionally, he might sound a little confused."

"Confused?"

"Only because he's tired. Really tired. When he's like that, he tends to wander. Today, I found him around the corner, messing with a neighbor's recycling bin."

"I think it was my bin."

"You live in that new house around the corner? That mansion?" She sounded envious.

"Yes, that's our place."

"Cost you the big bucks, didn't it?" Her eyes twinkled.

"I guess. My husband handles all that." Her intense glare felt uncomfortable, as did her interest in our finances.

"You've got that fancy red sports car, don't you? I see you driving around in it."

"It's a used BMW. My husband picked it up for a second car."

"Still, I'd love to have a convertible like that. Driving with the top down. The wind in your hair."

Fortunately, the tea kettle whistled. Enid's back was to me while she poured hot water into the mugs. The distraction gave me a chance to get the conversation back on track.

"Like I said, I'm worried about Bart. Windshield fluid bottles got dumped into our recycling bin. That liquid can be poisonous."

"Oops." She spilled a little water. Grabbing a towel, she mopped it up.

"I didn't realize you lived in that big place. Of course, you said you'd just moved in, when we first met, but I didn't know exactly which house was yours. It's not like you invited us — or me — to come over." She turned with the mugs in her hands. The look on her face was pretend hurt. "That wasn't very neighborly of you."

I felt uncomfortable and used taking the mug to cover up my

feelings. Why hadn't I invited her to visit? Well, first of all, because my house was a disaster. Secondly, I assumed that any invitation would be an interruption of her responsibilities as Mr. Bergen's caregiver.

A mean voice in my head suggested another reason: I hadn't invited her, because I didn't like her. I hadn't felt comfortable with Enid from the start. As I stirred sugar into my tea, my stomach twisted into a knot.

"I didn't invite you, because I couldn't offer you hospitality, like this. We moved in right after construction, so there was sawdust on every surface. The place is still full of boxes, but I am making headway. I'd love to have you. What times are you available?"

She sat back and regarded me with an unreadable face, as blank as a plain piece of copier paper. "I can do whatever I want, whenever I want."

"Oh, I figured you worked shifts, taking care of Mr. Bergen."

"Actually, it's Dr. Bergen." Her tone changed. There was an edge to it. "You do realize that, don't you? He's a very famous chemist. An important man. As for my schedule, I am free to come and go as I please. Maybe you didn't hear our news? Talbot and I are getting married. I'll never have to work again." With that, she shoved her left hand my way. A honking big diamond twinkled at me.

"Congratulations! Gee, I didn't know. That's big news. How exciting for you both."

She stared at me a bit longer, as if assessing whether I was serious or not. Once satisfied that I was sincere, her shoulders relaxed and her mouth curved into a self-satisfied smile. "It is a really big stone, isn't it? Knocks your eyes out. Cost a bundle."

"Boy, I had it all wrong. I thought you were his caregiver. Isn't that silly?"

She cocked her head and studied me. "That's how we met,

but he and I had a special connection right from the start."

"Wow. That's like a fairytale with a happy ending and all." I sipped my tea. Despite all the sugar I'd added, it was amazingly bad, very bitter, and that reminded me of my reason for visiting. "Before I forget, let's talk about the cat. Someone dumped a bunch of empty windshield fluid bottles into my recycling bin."

"Are you accusing Dr. Bergen?" Her nostrils flared, and her voice took a hike.

"No." I answered quickly, eager to calm her down. "Not at all. I just don't want Bart or some other pet to lap up any spilled fluid or lick the bottles. They could get sick or die."

"Why would they do that? Get into that stuff?"

"I guess the fluid is sweet. That's what I've been told."

"But the caps are on the bottles. How could an animal get the caps off?"

"Beats me. Chew them off? I suppose there might be traces around the mouth of the bottle. Maybe even liquid that has trickled down and dried on the outside. I imagine it wouldn't take much to hurt a pet."

"Hmmm. Sounds like I need to find that stupid cat and keep him inside the house. What time do they usually pick up the recycling? Why don't you just keep your stuff inside until they come?"

"Here's the thing. Those weren't our bottles. I don't know how they got in our bin. What if more bottles show up? What if there are other bottles out there in our neighborhood, and the cat finds them? I think you need to keep him inside. At least for a while."

"I doubt there's any problem." Enid picked up her cup and carried it to the sink. She rinsed it with such fervor that the water sprayed all over her and the counter. "But I guess, I'll have to go and look for him. That cat. He is a pain in my butt, for sure."

75

_I_ carried my cup and saucer to her sink. After I set them down, my phone rang. It was Robbie.

"Kiki? Where are you?"

"What do you mean?" I responded. Enid was watching me carefully.

"I'm in front of your house and you aren't answering the door."

"That's because I'm not at home."

"Where. Are. You?" He emphasized each and every word. "Right now? This instant?"

"Huh? I'm over here at the Bergens' house."

He swore under his breath. "Listen very carefully. Do not say my name out loud. Do not tell anyone who you've got on the line. Get out of there now. Right now. Make some excuse and get out! I'll meet you on the sidewalk."

"Okay." I ended the call, glancing up to see Enid. She was staring at me with such a hateful look.

"Who was that?" she demanded.

A sixth sense told me that I needed a reasonable excuse. I wasn't sure what was happening. I had no idea why Robbie was so frazzled. I shrugged. "A friend of my mother-in-law. She's incredibly bossy. You wouldn't believe how she treats me."

With an exaggerated sigh, I shoved my phone in my pocket. In the space of that brief call, Enid's body language had changed. Her eyes had hardened. Her face shut down, and her hands balled into fists.

Instinctively, I knew that I was in danger. I didn't know how or why, but I could feel it. Willing my face to stay blank, I reviewed my options quickly. My goal was to find common ground — a way to prove she and I were equals. "You would not believe the family I married into," I said as I rolled my eyes. "My husband's mother and her friends think they can boss me around. It's totally annoying. How do Dr. Bergen's daughters treat you?"

For a second, I didn't think it would work. But slowly, Enid relaxed.

"They treat me like dirt." She snorted angrily. Shaking her head, she added, "When we first met, they didn't have any time for him at all. Couldn't be bothered with dear old dad. But after they heard we were getting married, it's phone call after phone call. They're all sweetness and light with him. But with me? It's one threat after another. Huh."

"First they ignore him, now they're all over him, huh? What right do they have, sticking their noses into your business?"

"That's what I say. I make him happy. Serves them right for ignoring him. Mark my words, a lot of people are going to sit up and take notice. People who did me dirty. They'll get their come-uppance."

"What goes around, comes around," I said as I edged toward the hallway where the front door was in sight. "Hey, this has been delightful. I can't wait to have you over."

My nose is pug, but I felt it growing with every lie. For good measure, I added, "Of course, as a new bride, you'll probably be busy. Changing the décor and all."

"You've got that right. I'm going to dump all this boring stuff. Change things up. New furniture. The works."

I inched toward the doorway. The knob was two inches from my fingertips. "Thanks so much for your hospitality."

"Really?" She arched an eyebrow.

I froze. If I moved too fast, it would look like I was fleeing. I didn't want to spook her. "Yes, really. I feel like I've made a new friend."

Enid gave me an unsure smile. "Right. Me, too."

I touched the handle, but that cold metal reminded me why I'd come. "How about if I go through the garage instead? We could check to see if Bart's hiding there. Maybe between the two of us, we can grab him. I'd hate for him to get sick."

She studied me.

"It's up to you, of course." It sounded a bit lame, but I was putting control back in Enid's court.

"Right this way." She waved me down a hallway.

The garage door rumbled as it rolled open. Bright sunshine streamed in, blinding me. "Kitty-kitty-kitty?" I called out.

Enid stood next to Talbot's older model Saab. She leaned against it with her arms crossed over her chest. I'd expected her to join me in calling for the cat, too, but she didn't. Instead, she watched me carefully.

"K-k-k-kitty?" I walked in a slow circuit around the garage. Noting the industrial strength shelving packed with boxes designated as old clothes, paperwork, containers of bug spray, motor oil, and so on. Dropping to my knees, I looked under the car.

"K-k-k-kitty?" The word sounded extra sorrowful, because I was giving up hope. Returning to my feet, I shook my head. "Don't see him. Oh, well. At least I tried. See you soon, okay?"

She hit the garage door button and grabbed my arm. Her

strength surprised me. I was her captive. My heart fluttered with fear. Putting her mouth close to my ear, she said, "You see? I got nothing to hide. Nothing!"

"I never said you did! I was just trying to help you find your cat!"

Why, oh, why hadn't I gone directly out like Robbie had told me to do?

"You're nosy." It came out like a angry hiss. She tightened her grip on me.

"Maybe, but I'm more worried about Bart. I don't want a dead cat showing up in my garage, and I'm sure you don't want one either! Can you imagine the smell? And wouldn't that upset Dr. Bergen?"

Just as suddenly, she let me go. The odd glitter in her eyes seemed to fade away. "Dead cat. Yeah, you're right. He wouldn't like that."

"See? I was only trying to do you a favor."

"I want you out of my house." She pushed me into the hallway and toward the front door. Opening it with one hand, she said to me, "Get out and don't come back."

Enid gave me a little shove that sent me careening over the threshold. Rather than fall down the stairs, I gripped the wrought iron railing with both hands. The Bergens' front door closed behind me with a loud thump. But I did not hear the comforting snick that would confirm Enid had locked the door behind me.

And that spooked me.

As promised, Robbie Holmes stood at the end of the block, next to his police cruiser. He held a microphone pressed against his mouth. When he spotted me, he gestured that I should hurry toward him. The passenger side door of his car stood open, offering me a safe haven. I was afraid to run. What if Enid came after me?

Instead, I forced myself to walk at a quick, but casual, pace.

When I reached the cruiser, I threw myself inside and slammed the door. My heart banged around in my chest, threatening to break my ribs. Robbie climbed in, shut his door, and hit the locking mechanism.

"Whew," he said. "That was a close one."

I buried my head in my hands. "You're telling me."

76

"*Y*ou're okay now." Robbie reached over and patted me on the shoulder.

What followed was the world's shortest car ride. He backed up, turned his cruiser around, passed the vacant lot, and pulled into my driveway. A Ladue police cruiser sat in front of my house, directly across from the Nordstroms.

Everbright was behind the wheel of that car. As soon as Robbie gave him the thumbs up, Everbright drove past us, heading the way we'd come. Three more Ladue police cars came racing out of nowhere with lights flashing. They turned into the subdivision, following Everbright.

"Let's get you back into your house," said Robbie.

Car doors slammed in the distance. My hands shook, making the act of getting the key up into the lock a test of dexterity. Finally, the door swung open to reveal a very protective Zoe.

The fur stood up on her back as she barked and growled at my guest.

"No, no," I said, as I led her by the collar into the kitchen. "He's a friend."

After checking Robbie out, she calmed right down.

"When did you get a dog?" asked Robbie.

"She belongs to Brita Morgenstern. I'm watching her because Leesa Nordstrom doesn't like animals. I do."

Robbie pulled up a kitchen chair; I knew the drill. I measured grounds and water into the pot. Once the coffeemaker was doing its thing, I turned to the cop and asked, "Okay, why am I scared half-to-death? I know something is wrong, but I can't tell you what it is. And what was that nonsense with all the cop cars? The ones from Ladue?"

"Give it a minute, and I'll explain," he said. "But for future reference, always trust your instincts. Always. Your gut will never lie to you. You got out of there and that's the important thing."

I set the sugar bowl, the cream pitcher, and cups on the table. Robbie's phone rang. He answered, listened, nodded his head, and ended the call. "Got her."

"Her? You mean Enid?" I took a chair myself, while keeping my eyes on the slowly percolating coffee. The aroma of hazelnut scented the air.

"Enid James, also known as, Edith Janson, Evelyn Jordon, and other aliases. Wanted for extortion, fraud, theft, and other charges. A scam artist, who typically targets senior citizens, but also preys on other trusting souls."

"You do know that she's engaged to Talbot Bergen, don't you?" I got up and poured coffee. Opening the freezer, I found the last box in my stash of frozen Girl Scout Thin Mint cookies. Although I hated sharing them, good manners won over self-ishness.

"You sure about that?" Robbie frowned. "That they're engaged to be married?"

"Positive. She showed me her ring. A big, honking diamond."

"I'll pass that along." He sighed. "Dr. Bergen's daughters have been trying for weeks to get in touch with him, calling, knocking on the door, sending letters, dispatching friends to contact him, whatever. To no avail. Ms. James has blocked them at every turn. Finally they called social services. That's how the Ladue police got involved. You happened to be in the wrong place at the wrong time. Sheila and I were talking on the phone, when she mentioned you were home alone. She was worried about you. I dropped by, discovered you weren't home, but your car was here, and I assumed the worst."

"Sheila? Worried about me?" That was a shock.

"With Sven's killer on the loose, yes, she was."

"What will happen next?" My whole body sagged with relief. Would Enid really have hurt me? I wasn't sure. Turning my arm over, I saw the imprint of her fingers from where she'd grabbed me.

"Mr. Bergen's oldest daughter, Nancy, is waiting at the police station. Once she gets the all clear, she plans to go in and see to her father's welfare. She's already sworn out a restraining order designed to keep Ms. James from setting foot on the property. Nancy Bergen Stevens is rightly worried about her father's mental state. She knows he's suffering from dementia. But it might have gotten worse. The first step will be getting him to a doctor and having him checked over."

I nibbled a Thin Mint. "But none of this clears Brita Morgenstern."

Robbie raised a curious eyebrow at me. "I never said it would. Look, I know you have a kind heart, but facts are facts. She did it, Kiki. Killed her half-brother. Mrs. Morgenstern stands to inherit a lot of money. Immediately after her brother died, Brita Morgenstern demanded that Leesa Nordstrom release the body to her. That's a common tactic. The poisoner opts for cremation to destroy evidence. See? Everbright has a great case."

Zoe lifted her paw and set it on my thigh. When Brita's name was mentioned, the Lab flexed her nails, digging them into my leg. The dog's brown eyes focused on me exclusively, almost to the point of being creepy.

How could I help Brita?

In the distance, I heard the rumble of a truck. I jumped out of my chair and ran to my front window. The recycling truck was rounding the corner, coming toward our house. Throwing the door open, I headed for the blue recycling bin. The sigh of hydraulic brakes told me the crew was on the job. They pulled up next to my driveway and stopped. A man jumped down.

"Stop!" I yelled, standing over my discards with outstretched arms.

"Kiki?" Robbie stepped outside of my house.

"Robbie? Get over here and grab this." I pointed to the box in my curbside bin.

"I can pick that stuff up for you, ma'am," the recycling guy offered politely.

"Thanks but no thanks. Please, don't touch any of it. Robbie? You need to see this. Grab that sealed box. You can open it."

Robbie tore off the tape. "That's a lot of windshield fluid bottles. They all yours?"

The truck pulled away from the curb, and I shouted over the noise of the engine. "Nope. None of those bottles are ours. That's why you'll want to take them."

"You sure?" Robbie lifted the box and carried it to his car.

"Positive. I even checked with George. They didn't come from him. In fact, when I first dragged the recycling out, it was nearly empty. I'd filled the tub myself so I know what was in there. But then, someone came by and dumped all these windshield fluid bottles in the bin. Enid told me she found Dr. Bergen messing with my recycling."

"Really?" Robbie raised an eyebrow.

"I don't trust her. You don't either, do you? Is that what they found in Sven Nordstrom's body? Windshield washer fluid? You never said."

Instead of answering my question, Robbie countered with one of his own. "What made you worry about the bottles? Why did you concern yourself with them?"

"I didn't. Not initially. Mert noticed them as she was leaving. She'd gone with me to get Zoe. I told her about Bart, Dr. Bergen's cat. She realized that an animal might get sick if it licked up the fluid, so she called me from her truck to warn me. I looked up windshield washer fluid and discovered how lethal it can be. That's how Sven died, right? Windshield washer fluid in his Gatorade?"

Robbie stroked his chin and stared down at the box. "I won't talk about the investigation."

"These must have something to do with Sven's murder. It's gotta be!"

"Let me call a crime scene unit. We'll need a bona fide change of custody, in case Everbright wants to use this."

Doing a little victory dance, I pumped my fists and cheered. "I guessed it, didn't I?"

My feeling of satisfaction was short-lived, as I realized that I had been holding back. In my eagerness to be a good friend to our environment, I had hidden the murder weapon.

77

One week later...

"Let me get this straight." Mert set aside her mop and looked over her work. The hallway floor was finally clean and the tiles gleamed. "You had a Gatorade bottle in your car, this whole time? And it was the murder weapon?"

"Yup. Can you believe it?" I stepped back to admire our great room, the books were in the bookshelves, the furniture all in place, the coffee table perfectly situated, and everything looked terrific. "When Sven collapsed and lost his grip on his bike, that particular plastic bottle was knocked out of the holder. It wound up in the gutter. After the EMTs carted Sven away, I picked up the bottle, because I hate litter. I tossed it into my car, intending to put it in with our recycling. Then I forgot all about it. A lucky mistake, I guess. I wish I could claim credit for thinking that through, but I didn't."

"Sakes alive." Mert smirked at me. "Grabbing evidence and

holding onto it? That's perverting the course of justice. Could you wind up in jail?"

"Thank goodness, no. In fact, Robbie Holmes gave me this." I reached into my pocket and withdrew a child-sized badge. "He said I have a bright future in crime detection. Isn't that funny?"

Mert gave me an odd look, one that suggested she was uncomfortable with his suggestion, and then she smiled. "I'd say you want to steer clear of cops in the future. Mark my words, they ain't all nice like Deputy Chief Holmes is. Once't you get on their radar, you're sunk."

"I promise to stay away from cops in the future."

"You swear?" With a damp cloth, Mert finished mopping up the last of the dust and dirt from the baseboards.

"I swear." I held up three fingers, as if I was going to make a Girl Scout pledge.

She nodded her acknowledgement.

Turning my back to her, I reached into the last box and pulled out a picture of Anya right after she was born. There were dust fingerprints clouding the glass and silver frame. I walked into my kitchen to grab a bottle of Windex.

"Cops are sneaky as all get out. I'll hold you to that promise of yours. Steer clear of them. More trouble than they're worth. But you've still got some explaining to do. How come Enid wanted Sven Nordstrom dead? What did he ever do to her? I know the Nordstroms let her go, but I never did hear why."

"Enid got ahold of the Nordstroms' pin number and drained one of their checking accounts. She claimed that they owed her the money for working overtime. The amount wasn't that large, so they settled out of court. It happened right before Leesa hired you." I inspected the surface of the mirror I'd been cleaning. I'd learned from Mert that if you changed your vantage point, you could often see smudges.

"How'd Enid wind up over at Dr. Bergen's house?"

"Because she was working for the Nordstroms when it happened, Enid knew all about Alma's death. In fact, the minute Talbot Bergen became a widower, Enid started cozying up to him. Dropping by to see him. Baking special treats, and so on. When she realized his daughters weren't as involved as they should be, she applied for a job as one of his home healthcare workers. They're always looking for people at those agencies. As you might guess, it's hard work and low pay. Once Enid was part of the rotation, she gained Talbot's trust. Told him sob stories about how hard her life had been. Introduced him to her son. Made him feel special. Systematically, she cut him off from his daughters."

Mert stopped to grab a sip from her water bottle. "And then Enid convinced Talbot Bergen to poison Sven?"

"Right. She reminded him that Sven was responsible for Alma's accident. It was like picking at the emotional scab. See, Talbot Bergen really, really loved his wife. Her death devastated him. Enid kept telling Talbot that Sven had gotten away with murder. She encouraged him to get revenge. She's the one who mixed the windshield fluid into the Gatorade. After all, she knew Sven's habits. Once the bottles were tainted, Enid told Talbot to walk over and put them inside the refrigerator in the Nordstroms' garage. That way she wouldn't get caught red-handed where she didn't belong. He had the perfect alibi, searching for Bartholomew."

Mert handed me a bottle of water. "Then which one of them's guilty? Or are both of them? Enid or Dr. Bergen?"

"Nobody knows for sure. Talbot Bergen is definitely suffering from Alzheimer's. I'm not sure how competent he'll be to stand trial. His daughters have hired an attorney. Enid's hired a lawyer, too. She isn't saying much, but Robbie's pretty confident she'll cop a plea. She might even accuse Talbot of being the mastermind. "

"Will he go to jail?"

"Robbie thinks Dr. Bergen will be too confused to testify accurately, much less honestly." I chugged the water. Funny to think of how a simple plastic bottle could become a murder weapon. I walked it to the recycling tub we keep in the kitchen. "There's still one question left unanswered: *Why does the Nordstroms' garage door keep going up by itself?* If it hadn't been up so often, Talbot Bergen wouldn't have had access to the Nordstroms' refrigerator."

"I bet I know!" yelled Mert's son, Roger, from around the corner. He'd been babysitting Anya in the formal living room, playing with her while we worked. I was happy to pay the eight year old. Anya adored him, and he was a great kid.

"Really?" I stuck my head around the corner and asked him, "What's your theory, Roger?"

"While we've been playing, I've been watching that garage door. Guess what? Airplanes make it go up."

"Airplanes?" I repeated.

"Airplanes?" George came downstairs. He'd been hanging pictures and generally being helpful. After learning that one of our neighbors was a murdering con woman who'd put bruises on my arm, my husband had become incredibly protective. Robbie had given George a stern talking to, pointing out that his unpredictable schedule had put Anya and me at risk. The fact that I'd cleared his name also made George realize he should be more grateful to me. And, yes, I also suspected that Mert had given him a piece of her mind or, at the very least, a tongue lashing.

George stared out the front window as he considered Roger's idea. "There's one way to find out. A guy I went to high school with is an engineer at McDonnell Douglas, I'll call him and ask."

In two minutes, we had our answer.

"You are one smart kid, Roger. Turns out that it's possible some planes emit a signal on the same radio frequency as the Nordstroms' garage door opener. It's certainly happened before. Give me a high five, buddy." George raised his open palm so Roger could slap it.

"That there garage door's been going up by itself ever since the Nordstroms moved into that house." Mert tucked a dust rag into her belt loop. As a housekeeper, she had proved herself to be without equal. Not only did she know how to clean anything and everything, but she tackled any mess with an energy that impressed me.

As a friend of the family, she was quickly becoming indispensable.

"That is so weird!" I said. "I asked Sven why they kept leaving the door up. He was irritated by my question. According to him, they didn't leave the door up — and I guess that was true. But the planes on their way to the airport must have triggered the opener."

"And that explains how Talbot Bergen was able to walk right into the Nordstorms' garage and poison the Gatorade." Mert laughed, but her chuckle wasn't one of amusement. Instead, she sounded sad. "Who'd have thunk it?"

78

A few weeks later, Anya was playing happily with a new toy that re-created sounds that animals make. Oh, how she loved critters! Her favorite was the dog, a black Lab. "Zo-oh?" she would ask, over and over, pointing to the cartoon image.

Rather than remind her that Zoe had gone away, probably forever, I would say, "Yes, sweetheart. Zoe is a dog."

The doorbell rang and the postman handed me a small mailing box. After thanking him, I glanced over at the tall grasses that divided our lot from the Bergens' yard. I missed Bart. It seemed like a long time ago that he was slinking through the weeds.

After Talbot Bergen was moved to a facility that specialized in memory care, I'd had high hopes we could give Bartholomew a new home. When I asked Robbie about the animal, he told me that Talbot Bergen's oldest daughter had claimed the long-haired black cat. The young woman had promised to give the wandering feline a good home.

Maybe it was for the best. Bart was a rascal. Keeping him indoors would have been a challenge.

I turned my attention to the box. The postmark showed it had been mailed from Minnesota. I love, love, love surprises, especially if they are gifts! With trembling fingers, I pried open the flaps.

Inside was a small photo frame displaying a picture of Brita and the wonderful Zoe. Underneath was a tiny pillow with a miniscule pocket trimmed in lace. French knots spelled out "Tooth Fairy." The note inside said:

Dear Kiki and Anya,

Please accept this small remembrance of our time together, and think of me kindly. I laid Sven's ashes to rest last week. Thanks to you, justice was done.

Zoe sends her love, as do I.

Brita

***

KIKI'S STORY CONTINUES WITH...
Paper, Scissors, Death: Book #1 in the Kiki Lowenstein Mystery Series

A SPECIAL GIFT FOR YOU

I am deeply appreciative of all my readers, and so I have a special gift for you. It's a full-length digital book called *Bad, Memory, Album.* Just go here and tell me where to send your digital book https://dl.bookfunnel.com/jwu6iiperg.
All best always,
Joanna

For any book to succeed, reviews are essential. If you enjoyed this book please leave a review on Amazon. A sentence or two can make all the difference! Please leave a review of *Love, Die, Neighbor* here http://www.Amazon.com/review/create-review?& asin=B074KPYTJ2

THE KIKI LOWENSTEIN MYSTERY SERIES

BY JOANNA CAMPBELL SLAN

Every scrapbook tells a story. Memories of friends, family and … murder? You'll want to read the Kiki Lowenstein books in order: Kiki Lowenstein Mystery Series - https://amzn.to/38VkBjW

Looking for more enjoyable reads? Joanna has a series just for you!

Cara Mia Delgatto Mystery Series, a traditional cozy mystery series with witty heroines, and former flames reconnecting, set in Florida's beautiful Treasure Coast - https://amzn.to/30z9urN

The Jane Eyre Chronicles, Charlotte Bronte's Classic Strong-Willed Heroine Lives On. – **https://amzn.to/3r3Ybmd**

The Confidential Files of John H. Watson, a new series featuring Sherlock Holmes and John Watson. - https://amzn.to/3bDnSWo

About the author...
Joanna Campbell Slan

Joanna is a *New York Times* and a *USA Today* bestselling author who has written more than 40 books, including both fiction and non-fiction works. She was one of the early Chicken Soup for the Soul authors, and her stories appear in five of those *New York Times* bestselling books. Her first non-fiction book, ***Using Stories and Humor: Grab Your Audience*** (Simon & Schuster/Pearson), was endorsed by Toastmasters International, and lauded by Benjamin Netanyahu's speechwriter. She's the author of four mystery series. Her first novel—***Paper, Scissors, Death: Book #1 in the Kiki Lowenstein Mystery Series***—was shortlisted for the Agatha Award. Her first historical mystery—***Death of a Schoolgirl: Book #1 in the Jane Eyre Chronicles***—won the Daphne du Maurier Award of Excellence. Her contemporary series set in Florida continues this year with ***Ruff Justice Book #5 in the Cara Mia Delgatto Mystery Series***. Her fantasy thriller series starts with ***Sherlock Holmes and the Giant Sumatran Rat***.

In addition to writing fiction, Joanna edits the Happy Homicides Anthologies and has begun the Dollhouse Décor & More series of "how to" books for dollhouse miniaturists.

Joanna independently published ***I'm Too Blessed to be Depressed*** back in 2004 when she was working as a motivational speaker. She sold more than 34,000 copies of that title. Since then she's gone on to independently publish a full-color book, ***The Best of British Scrapbooking,*** numerous digital books, and coloring books. Her book ***Scrapbook Storytelling*** sold 120,000 copies.

She's been an Amazon Bestselling Author too many times to count and has been included in the ranks of Amazon's Top 100 Mystery Authors.

A former talk show host and sought-after motivational speaker, Joanna has spoken to small and large (1000+) groups on four continents. *Sharing Ideas Magazines* named her "one of the top 25 speakers in the world."

When she isn't banging away at the keyboard, Joanna keeps busy walking her Havanese puppy Jax. An award-winning miniaturist, Joanna builds dollhouses, dolls, and furniture from scratch. She's also an accredited teacher of Zentangle®. Her husband, David, owns Steinway Piano Gallery-DC and five other Steinway piano showrooms.

Contact Joanna at JCSlan@JoannaSlan.com.

~

Follow her on social media by going here
https://www.linktr.ee/JCSlan